THE AGONY OF ALICE

OTHER YEARLING BOOKS YOU WILL ENJOY:

NIGHT CRY, *Phyllis Reynolds Naylor*
WITCH'S SISTER, *Phyllis Reynolds Naylor*
WITCH WATER, *Phyllis Reynolds Naylor*
FROM THE MIXED-UP FILES OF MRS. BASIL E. FRANKWEILER,
E. L. Konigsburg
JENNIFER, HECATE, MACBETH, WILLIAM MCKINLEY, AND ME,
ELIZABETH, *E. L. Konigsburg*
ANASTASIA AGAIN!, *Lois Lowry*
ANASTASIA, ASK YOUR ANALYST, *Lois Lowry*
ANASTASIA ON HER OWN, *Lois Lowry*
ANASTASIA AT YOUR SERVICE, *Lois Lowry*

YEARLING BOOKS/YOUNG YEARLINGS/YEARLING CLASSICS are designed especially to entertain and enlighten young people. Charles F. Reasoner, Professor Emeritus of Children's Literature and Reading, New York University, is consultant to this series.

For a complete listing of all Yearling titles,
write to Dell Readers Service,
P.O. Box 1045, South Holland, Illinois 60473.

The
AGONY
of
ALICE

by Phyllis Reynolds Naylor

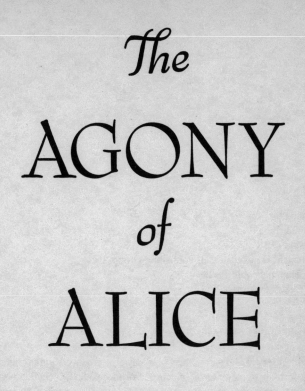

A Yearling Book

Published by
Dell Publishing
a division of
The Bantam Doubleday Dell Publishing Group, Inc.
1 Dag Hammarskjold Plaza
New York, New York 10017

Yearling® TM 913705, Dell Publishing, a division of
the Bantam Doubleday Dell Publishing Group, Inc.

ISBN: 0-440-40051-1

Reprinted by arrangement with Macmillan Publishing Company on behalf of Atheneum Publishers

Printed in the United States of America

May 1988

10 9 8 7 6 5 4 3 2

CW

To my sister Norma

Contents

THE AGONY OF ALICE

1

Kissing Tarzan

THE SUMMER between fifth and sixth grades, something happens to your mind. With me, the box of Crayolas did it—thirty-two colors including copper and burgundy. I was putting them in a sack for our move to Silver Spring when I remembered how I used to eat crayons in kindergarten.

I didn't just eat them, either. One day when I was bored I stuck two crayons up my nostrils, then leaned over my desk and wagged my head from side to side like an elephant with tusks, and the teacher said, "Alice McKinley, what on earth are you doing?"

Thinking about those crayons and that teacher was so embarrassing that it made my palms tingle, my neck hot. Surely, I thought, it was about the weirdest thing I'd ever done. And then, after I'd packed the Crayolas, I found a copy of a poem I had written in third grade:

> There are lots of drops in the ocean,
> There are lots of stars in the blue;
> But in the whole state of Maryland,
> There's only one person like you.

I stopped worrying about the crayons and cringed at the poem. Do you know who I wrote it for? My father? My grandfather? Aunt Sally? The milkman, when the company stopped home deliveries. Because he looked so sad when he told us. I hardly even knew him.

The reason I worry about my mind is that as soon as I remembered the milkman, I wondered if he was still alive, and somewhere, deep inside me, I sort of hoped he wasn't. I didn't want anybody remembering that poem. I wondered if my kindergarten teacher was alive, too. If I met her on the street tomorrow, would she still remember me as the girl with Crayolas up her nose? Those were absolutely the two most ridiculous things I had ever done in my life, I thought, and then I remembered this big piece of cardboard back in fourth grade and this boy named Donald Sheavers.

Donald was stupid and good-looking, and I liked him a lot.

"Come over and watch television, Donald," I'd say, and he'd come over and watch television. Any channel I wanted.

"I guess it's time for you to go home, Donald," I'd say later, and he'd go home.

I'll bet if I'd ever said, "Wear your clothes backwards, Donald," he'd have worn his clothes backwards. But I never asked him to do that because, as I said, I liked him. Then I found this big sheet of cardboard.

It came in a box with our Sears washing machine. Dad couldn't fix the old one and Lester's shirts kept coming out wrinkled, so this deluxe model arrived with the permanent press cycle and I got to keep the cardboard.

I was lying out on the grass in the shade on my cardboard looking up at the box elder and I remembered this old Tarzan movie I'd seen on TV. Tarzan and Jane were on a raft on the river, and they were kissing. They didn't know it, but the raft was getting closer and closer to a waterfall, and just before it went over the rocks, Tarzan grabbed hold of a vine, picked up Jane, and swung to shore. That was all. But suddenly I wanted to know what it felt like to be kissed on a raft with my life in danger. That's when I thought of Donald.

"Donald," I said when he came over, "you want to be in the movies?"

"Yes," said Donald. He even looked like Tarzan. He had dark hair and brown eyes, and he went around all summer in cut-offs.

I told him about the raft and the waterfall, and I sort of rushed through the part about kissing.

"We can't do it," Donald said. "We don't have a river."

"We'll just have to pretend that, Donald."

"We don't have a vine," he told me.

I got a rope and tied it to a branch in the box elder.

I was afraid he'd complain about the kissing next, but when the rope was ready, he said, "Okay. Let's do it."

And suddenly I thought of all kinds of things we had to do first. We had to be chased through the forest by pygmies, and then there was this quicksand and an alligator, but finally we made it to the raft, and Donald came crashing down beside me. I pushed him away.

"You have to get on the raft *gently*, Donald," I told him.

He came running again, grabbed the rope, and lowered himself onto the raft, but this time I rolled off.

"What's the matter?" asked Donald.

"I don't know," I said uncomfortably. "I think we have to start with the pygmies and sort of work into it."

We went back to the chase scene through the forest. Donald climbed the box elder and pounded his chest and bellowed. We leaped over the quicksand and over the alligator, and there we were on the raft once more.

This time I got the giggles. Donald did his part perfectly, but just when he got close enough that I could smell his breath—Donald always had a sort of stale bubble gum smell—I rolled off again.

For a whole afternoon we tried it. We added cannibals and burning torches and a gorilla, but somehow I could not get through the kissing. Donald laughed and thought it was a joke, but I was disgusted with myself.

It came to an end very quickly. I decided that I could not have any dinner that evening unless I got through the kissing scene. *This is it*, I thought as we ran through the forest with the gorilla grabbing at our heels. Donald swung around in the box elder yelping and beating his chest. Then the quicksand, the alligator, and the cardboard. Suddenly:

"Donald!" came my father's voice from the side window.

Donald rolled one way, and I rolled the other. The next thing I knew my Dad had come outside and was standing there in the grass.

"I don't think you should be doing that with Al," said my father. (I'm the only girl in our family, but he still calls me "Al.") "You'd better go home now, Donald, and the next time you come over, think of something better to do."

"Okay," said Donald.

All I did was sit there and stare at my knees. I didn't even tell Dad that the kissing was my idea, so Donald got the blame.

We didn't play Tarzan anymore that summer, and I never did get kissed on the raft. When school started and Donald passed me in the hall, sometimes he'd thump his chest and grin, just to tease me, but for the most part I forgot all about it. He became interested in basketball and I got interested in books, and I probably went through fifth grade without thinking of Donald more than a couple times.

That same afternoon, however, when I was getting ready to move and I dropped the Crayolas in the sack, I started remembering all the embarrassing things I had ever done in my life. The milkman might have died and my kindergarten teacher may have passed away, but Donald Sheavers was alive and well.

I began to wish that he wasn't. I didn't really want him to die or anything, just maybe quietly disappear so that the only person left who would remember any of the dumb things I'd ever done would be me. It was bad enough remembering them myself. Exactly one hour later, when I was packing my tinfoil collection, I heard that Donald Sheavers had fallen off his bike and had a brain concussion.

I didn't eat any dinner. I remembered that Donald was Catholic and I thought maybe if I prayed to one of the saints it might help. I thought maybe women saints helped girls and men saints helped boys, but the only saints I could think of were Saints Mary and Bernadette. Then I thought of a Saint Bernard dog. I figured there must be a Saint Bernard, so I sat down in a corner of my room and prayed. I told him that if I had ever let one little wish reach heaven about Donald Sheavers disappearing to please, *please*, disregard it and let Donald live.

"Sure you don't want any supper, Al?" Dad asked, but I said no.

"You worried about Donald Sheavers?"

I nodded. The next day when I didn't come down to breakfast, Dad called Mrs. Sheavers, and she said that Donald was better. In fact, she said, it would be perfectly fine if we went to the hospital to see him, so I bought a package of Necco wafers and Dad drove me over. I closed my eyes and prayed to Saint Bernard one last time. I thanked him for letting Donald live and asked if he could please fix it so that playing Tarzan back in fourth grade would be erased forever from Donald's mind.

The nurse directed us to room 315, and we went in. Donald was sitting up with a bandage around his forehead, sipping a milkshake. He was still good-looking, even with the bandage. Donald grinned at me, set the milkshake down, and just as I was about to hand him the Necco wafers, he pounded his chest and gave a Tarzan yell.

I found out later that there are a lot of Saint Bernards, so I figure my prayer just got to heaven and sat around in the dead-letter box.

The movers came the next morning, and we left Takoma Park for Silver Spring, a few miles away. I was glad. I wanted to start a whole new life with different people. But we had only been in the new house five hours and fifteen minutes before I embarrassed my whole family.

2

Agnes Under the Mattress

WE'VE MOVED three times in my life, but I only remember two times. We moved from Tennessee to Chicago before I was born, from Chicago to Takoma Park, Maryland, when I was six, and from Takoma Park to Silver Spring when I was eleven. I've never had many relatives around. Most of mine are in Tennessee, and we don't visit unless someone dies or gets married or something.

I had an Uncle Charlie who married when he was fifty-seven and died two days later. We'd just driven back to Maryland and had to turn around and go to Tennessee again to bury him. At the funeral dinner there was this sort of weird-looking cake that they called lemon sponge, but I knew it was just leftover wedding cake with sauce on it.

All the McKinleys call each other on Christmas morning, though—the Tennessee contingent calls us in Silver Spring. ("Silver Sprangs," Uncle Howard calls it.) Everybody down there says "Merry Christmas" to everyone up here, which is sort of nice because it means they care about us. Dad says lots of people care about me and I don't even know it; but if you don't know it, I tell him, what's the point?

"Don't you even remember Aunt Sally?" he says.

Whenever I try to remember Aunt Sally, though, Dad gets upset.

"Is she the one who used to read me the Little Bear books?" I say.

And Dad says, "Al, that was your *mother*." He takes off his glasses and looks at me hard. "That was your *mother*!" he says again in case I hadn't heard.

Momma died when I was four, and I can only remember bits and pieces; but I mix her up with Aunt Sally, because we lived in Chicago then. Some of the time, in fact, I even mix her up with Sally's husband, Uncle Milt, and that *really* fractures my dad.

The trouble with all this is I never quite know exactly who I'm supposed to be like or how I'm supposed to act. What I need, I guess, is a pattern, a road map; but all I've got is a father and Lester, and Lester has been no help to me whatsoever.

I remember once when I was seven hearing some older girls talking about their periods.

"Lester," I said, "what's a period?"

"A comma without the tail," said Lester. He was fifteen at the time, but even I knew that girls wouldn't spend a whole recess talking about commas.

I was thinking about Momma the day I found the picture of Saint Agnes in our new neighborhood. It was lying out on the sidewalk and had a big shoe print on top of it, but I rubbed it on my jeans and took it up on the porch.

It was sort of like a picture postcard, the kind that Catholics carry around, and I figured it belonged to Elizabeth Price. She lives across the street from us here in Silver Spring and knows all about saints. (We're Methodists, and the only thing I know that Elizabeth doesn't is a couple of hymns.)

I rocked back and forth on the glider and studied the card. "The Agony of Saint Agnes," it said at the top with lilies all around it. There was a drawing of a very beautiful girl with long dark hair like Elizabeth's. She had a lamb in one arm and a palm branch in the other, and she was looking up to heaven.

Underneath the picture was her story. It said that Agnes was only twelve years old at the time of her glorious death. Her beauty excited the young noblemen of Rome, and one even promised to save her if she would marry him and renounce her faith, but she would not and was cruelly whipped. Even the pagans wept to see her tortured so. At last she was put to death and is looked upon in the Church as a special patroness of bodily purity.

I don't know what there was about Saint Agnes, but I liked her. I figured I might need her more than Elizabeth Price, so I took the picture upstairs and hid it under my mattress. If Elizabeth was ever in difficulty, though, I'd take it over.

When you walk in Elizabeth's house, the first thing you see is this big photograph over the sofa of Elizabeth on her Confirmation day. She has on this white dress with lace around the collar and these white gloves with lace around the wrists and a white veil. Her long dark hair is all shiny around her shoulders, and she's looking down at a bunch of flowers. She even looks like a saint. I asked Elizabeth once what you had to do to be a saint, and she said you had to die first, so then I stopped thinking about it so much. But I still kept Saint Agnes under my mattress just in case.

It was Elizabeth Price who watched us move in. She was sitting on a wicker couch on her front porch with her mother, and they were reading a magazine together except that they never turned the pages. That's how I knew they were watching us. It's really creepy, you know, when someone watches you move in. I had on my oldest clothes and my socks didn't match, and even from across the street I could tell that Elizabeth Price had on brand new sneakers.

It took us all day to get things inside. The movers took the furniture, but Dad and Lester and I took the really important things in our car. Dad had the lampshades and I had my bowl of guppies and Lester had his beer can collection, which reached from the floor to the ceiling all along one wall of his room. He sold it just before he started junior college this year and got two hundred and sixty-eight dollars.

It was a gorgeous day in July, and it could have been the marvelous very first day of the rest of my life, like the posters tell you. I was feeling especially good because Dad had promised to take us to Shakey's for pizza after the movers left, so I was being as helpful as I possibly could. I helped Lester set up his beer cans and put lampshades on all the lamps and fed the guppies and dusted the closets, thinking all the time about pepperoni or sausage and a king-sized mug of 7-Up.

But just as the moving van pulled away, someone knocked, and I knew even before I opened the door that it was going to be that girl across the street and her mother.

They were standing there in matching skirts holding a cardboard box, and I didn't even have to look inside to know that it was supper. My heart fell.

"Welcome to the neighborhood," said the girl, smiling at me, and she didn't have braces, either. She had beautiful hair and beautiful long eyelashes and no braces.

"Thanks," I told her.

"We're the Prices, and this is Elizabeth," her mother said. "We know how difficult it is on moving day, so we brought you some dinner." She held out the box for me to see. There was a meatloaf, which I hate, some baked potatoes, a salad, and a plate of flat-looking brownies, which I bet Elizabeth made herself.

"I made those myself," said Elizabeth, pointing.

I didn't know what to say. The dinner was hot and ready to be eaten, and I thought maybe they could give it to someone else.

"Thanks a lot," I told them, "but we're going out to dinner."

"Alice!" my dad said behind me, and came right over. "This was so nice of you," he told them, taking the box. "Thank you very much. I'm sure we'll enjoy it. I'm Ben McKinley and this is Alice."

"If you need anything," said Elizabeth's mother, "we're just across the street."

We ate off a trunk in the living room. Dad and Lester kept forking the food down like it was the best thing they had eaten in years, but I could hardly swallow.

"This tastes like dead birds," I said.

Dad frowned at me. "That was a very rude thing you told them, after all their work. . . ."

"But you *promised*!" I protested. "The dinner was still hot, and I figured they could give it to the needy or something. . . ."

"They didn't make it for the needy, they made it for us," Dad told me. "We can go to Shakey's some other time."

"Yeah, Al," said Lester. "You really blew it."

I got up and went to brush my teeth, only we hadn't unpacked the toothbrushes so I had to use my finger. That was when I noticed the dirt smudges on my face and the mustard on my shirt from lunch. I guess I'd forgotten to brush my hair that morning too, and it hung all dirty-yellow and stringy around my shoulders. I could imagine what Elizabeth Price was thinking about me.

Life is like a dumpster. As soon as you get rid of one embarrassment, you pick up another. I knew that this was going to go on forever unless I found someone to set an example for me, and by the time I got the mustard off my shirt, I'd made up my mind: I'd adopt a mother, and she wouldn't even know.

3
Lips Together, Teeth Apart

I DON'T understand about Lester. I would think he'd be so grateful to have a road map he'd just follow everything my father did. Instead, Lester does the opposite. It's like having a road map, I guess, and reversing directions.

My father is manager of a music store on Georgia Avenue. It's part of a chain, the Melody Inn. Back in Tennessee he was a clerk. In Chicago, he was an instructor. But when they transferred him to Maryland, they made him manager. On weekends around the house he wears a white tee shirt that says "Happy Birthday, Beethoven" in black letters. Lester wears a black tee shirt that reads "Surf Naked."

Dad plays the violin and the flute. Lester plays an electric guitar. Dad drinks white wine in a thin goblet with a long glass stem. Lester drinks Budweiser from a can. Dad reads things like *The Letters of Gustave Flaubert 1830–1857*. Lester reads the comics.

I asked Dad once what it was about Lester, and Dad said he was out to lunch.

"What?" I asked.

"He's out to lunch, but he'll be home for supper," Dad said, and I knew he was speaking in riddles again. Lately, however, Lester's been acting a little less weird, so maybe that's what Dad meant about coming home.

I had been looking forward to sixth grade all my life. It would be the very first time I was an "upper classman." There wouldn't be any older boys on the playground to trap me on the slide. There wouldn't be any older girls in the restroom to hide the toilet paper. Sixthgraders were always chosen to help out in the office or in the halls, and the only ambition I had in life that summer was to be a safety patrol when school started.

There were a few things that had to be done before September, however. Dad made an appointment for me with a new dentist.

It's weird about dentists. They always slip into the room so quietly you don't even know they're there until you hear them washing their hands at the sink. I'd been looking at a poster taped on the wall just in front of me. It had a big mince pie on it and the words, "Before you finish eating your dinner, your dinner starts eating your teeth."

The dentist came around from behind and sat down on a stool with his little mirror and his silver pick. I immediately opened my mouth. I always feel like a baby bird in a dentist's office. As soon as he comes near me, my mouth opens automatically. His fingers smelled like Novocain and all the while he was examining my teeth he was asking me questions. That's another thing about dentists. They ask you questions when your mouth's open and then they answer for you.

"Almost ready for school?" he said.

"Gaaauuu," I answered.

He told me that I didn't have any cavities, but that I must be grinding my teeth because the enamel was worn. People do that, he said, when they're tense. Then he recited a little poem that he hoped I would always remember:

> *"From this rule I won't depart,*
> *Lips together, teeth apart."*

I figured I'd forget it in a day or two, but it stuck in my head like library paste. When we went to church on Sunday, it followed me right into the hymn. The first two lines were:

> *"Love divine, all loves ex-celling,*
> *Joy of heav'n, to earth come down;"*

And long after the hymn was over and the minister had started the sermon, the dentist's rhyme kept ringing in my ears to the same tune:

> *"From this rule I won't de-pa-rt,*
> *Lips to-ge-ther, teeth a-part."*

On Monday, though, I turned my attention to clothes. My dad asked what I wanted to wear to sixth grade, and I told him I was tired of ordering my clothes from the Sears catalog. I wanted to go to one of those stores that sells Levis and get a real pair with the name on the pocket. Dad said that Lester would take me, so one afternoon we set off for a store that had light bulbs blinking on and off and rock music coming from a speaker.

My brother is nineteen and has a mustache. I asked him if girls like to kiss a man with a mustache and he asked if I wanted to find out and I said no. Lester and I don't say very much to each other, but when we do, it's right to the point.

Of course, there are some things we don't talk about at all. Like how to buy a bra. Not even Dad can talk about that. At the beginning of June, he noticed that my breasts made points in my tee shirts, so he said, "Al, don't you think you should be wearing something under that shirt?" I went upstairs and put on a second tee shirt over the first, and all summer long I wore two shirts at a time just to hide my points. All because I didn't know how to buy a bra.

I looked them up in the Sears catalog once, but there were nine pages about contour uplifts, fiberfill supports, underwire minimizers, DD cups, and something called the "Seamless Ah-h Bra." I mean, I couldn't even speak the language.

When we got to The Gap, I followed Lester inside

and stared helplessly at the bins of folded jeans that reached all the way to the ceiling. Each bin had two numbers on it, like 29-33 and 32-31.

Lester stuck his hands in his pockets and looked me over. "Well," he said finally, "I'm thirty-three, thirty-four, so I guess you're . . . oh, maybe twenty-nine, thirty."

I didn't know what the numbers meant, but Lester got down a pair of Levis for me. Then he took me to the row of dressing rooms in back and found one that was empty. I went in. There was no lock on the door. I went back out.

"What's the matter?" asked Lester.

"Hold the door," I told him.

Lester rolled his eyes and came over to lean on it.

I slipped off my Sears Toughskins and pulled on the Levis. They didn't even bend. I tried to imagine going to school in jeans that sounded like windshield wipers when you walked.

I stepped in one leg and then the other and promptly fell over. The jeans were so long my feet couldn't get out. I pulled them up around my ankles and stood up. There was enough room around the waist for a sofa cushion.

"Hey, Al," Lester was saying outside the door. "They fit?"

I opened the door a crack, and Lester stuck his head in.

"Stay here," he said when he saw me. "I'll get the smallest they've got."

I held onto the Levis until Lester brought back a pair that said 25-30. I tried them on. They still came down over my feet and I could stick both fists in the waist.

"I can't figure it out," said Lester. "Maybe you've got a strange body or something."

I felt like I had swallowed an ice cube. I was what I always suspected: a freak. Other girls my age wore jeans with Levis on the pocket, but I would never be able to wear them because I was obviously deformed. Tears sprang up in my eyes.

Have you ever had a perfectly rotten experience turn out wonderful? At that precise moment a salesgirl was passing the door and she looked in.

"How we doing?" she said, and checked the size. "For heaven's sake," she told Lester, "she should be wearing Levis from the girls' department." And with that she took my arm and guided me out to a huge rack of jeans just made for me.

If I had had a sister, she would have known. If I had had a mother, she would have asked. Instead, Lester told me I was strange and would have taken me back home in tears. I shot him a dirty look as I clutched a pair of jeans to my chest and marched triumphantly back to the dressing room.

Have you ever had a perfectly wonderful experience turn out awful? I opened the wrong door. There stood a red-haired boy in blue underpants. He wore white sport socks with yellow stripes around the tops and he was staring at me with his mouth open. I slammed the door as Lester pushed me into the right room, and I decided I would never come out as long as I lived. They could call the Rescue Squad, but I would stay in that dressing room forever. Miserably I tried on the size one jeans and they fit perfectly, but I was so embarrassed I couldn't even enjoy them.

"Al," Lester said finally. "You still alive?"

"I'm not coming out," I told him, "not ever."

"He's gone, Al."

"I can hear him breathing."

"He's *gone*. That's someone else."

I came out at last and went with Lester up to the cash register. There was the boy with the blue underpants in line just ahead of us. I stood behind Lester with my forehead pressed up against his back and didn't look up again until we were in the parking lot.

"When are you going to grow up?" Lester asked me.

"It was awful!" I told him. "It was so humiliating."

"It could have been worse," said Lester. "It could have been you standing there in your underpants and *he* opened the door."

I had a long, hard think about myself that night. I remembered a fairy tale I'd read once about a princess who worried all the time about getting old. One day her fairy godmother told her that if she really wanted, the godmother could fix it so that the princess grew younger instead of older. "Think about it for three days," the godmother said, and when she came back, the princess said yes, she really, truly, sincerely wanted to grow younger. So the princess got her wish. For the first couple years she was happy, but at the end of the story, she was lying in bed shaking a rattle and then she wasn't anything at all. I got to worrying that instead of growing up, I was growing more babyish all the time.

I got out one of the posters from behind my dresser—Dad saves them for me from the Melody Inn—and I turned it over and drew a line down the center. On the left side I wrote *Forward*, and on the right side I wrote *Backward*. In the "forward" column I scribbled down all the things I'd taught myself to do that showed I was growing up, and in the "backward" column I listed all the things I'd done that set me back a couple of years:

Forward	*Backward*
Make Kraft Dinner	Ate crayons
Empty lint trap on dryer	Wrote poem to milkman
Remove splinters	Donald Sheavers
Eat squash	Rude to Elizabeth Price
Raise guppies	Can't buy a bra
	Opened wrong door at Gap

So far the "backwards" were winning.

On September fifth, I went to school in my new Levis beside Elizabeth Price. She said that on the first day of school, all the students gather on the playground, and the teachers come out and call the names of those who will be in their classes.

It was chilly and I wished I'd worn my coat instead of a sweater. The patrol boy had his hood up on his jacket and he blew on his hands while he waited for a car to pass. I tried to imagine all of us standing there on the playground in the cold, waiting for our names to be called, like orphans waiting to be adopted or something.

When we reached the school, it was there, under the basketball net, that I saw the woman I wanted to be my adopted mother. She was one of the sixth grade teachers, Elizabeth told me, and her name was Miss Cole. She was tall and slim and simply gorgeous, with sandy hair curled under around the edge. She wore slacks that fit perfectly and a blue sweater, and she was holding a clipboard to her chest, joking with some of the students.

I couldn't take my eyes off her. She smiled the way I wanted to smile, laughed the way I wanted to laugh, looked the way I wanted to look, and I just knew that if I could only be in her classroom for one year, I would come out a beautiful new person with my hair curled under and would never do a dumb thing again as long as I lived.

Everyone was talking about which teacher they wanted to get. The boys wanted Mr. Weber who looked like a teddy bear with thick glasses. He was nice too, Elizabeth said, and always took his class on an overnight campout the last week of school.

And then, Elizabeth was saying in a whisper, there was Mrs. Plotkin.

I turned to where Elizabeth's eyes were looking and saw a human pear. Mrs. Plotkin was standing alone on the blacktop while the other teachers read off their lists. She was about sixty years old, and while she started out normal around the neck, her body grew wider and wider on the way down, as though all the fat had dropped somehow and gathered around her legs and ankles. Her dress was green and shapeless, and her gray hair hung short and straight on either side of her face.

I sucked in my breath as students gathered around Mr. Weber when he read off his list. Elizabeth looked relieved when her name was called and walked over to stand beside him. Mr. Weber went inside with his pupils, and Miss Cole began reading her list. My heart began to thump wildly when she reached the L's, then the M's:

"Patrick Long, Josephine Mackey, Ann Martin, Ted Norris. . . ."

I closed my eyes and swallowed. Maybe *nobody* had my name. Perhaps, when Dad registered me the week before, they had forgotten to put me down. When everyone had gone inside, I would go the principal and ask to be in Miss Cole's classroom.

I could tell by the sound of her voice that she was calling the last name on her list. And then, flashing a smile to her lucky students, Miss Cole led them inside.

I stood silently, my eyes on my feet, as Mrs. Plotkin

read off her list. Even her name was ugly. I simply could not bear to sit in her classroom for ten months. I could not bear to watch her waddle up to the blackboard, the fat on her arms swinging. I would get sick at my stomach. I would develop asthma. I would tell the principal I was allergic.

I heard her call my name.

I could have been in Mr. Weber's class, going on an overnight with my sleeping bag. I could have been in Miss Cole's class, learning to put on lip gloss. Instead, I was walking behind a pear-shaped woman whose rear was as wide as a yardstick.

I realized I was grinding my teeth. It would only be a matter of time, I promised, before Mrs. Plotkin expelled me from her class.

4
Plod-kin

FIRST, however, I decided to try something else. In the classroom, Mrs. Plotkin began seating us alphabetically in rows, and I knew that if I was ever going to be transferred, it would have to be right then, before there was a desk assigned to me.

My father knew a woman once who went to the hospital to have her right leg removed in an operation, and when she woke up the left leg was gone. She said later it did seem odd when they X-rayed the left leg the day before, but she figured they knew what they were doing.

"Let that be a lesson, Al," my father told me. "If you have something to say, don't put it off."

"Alice McKinley," Mrs. Plotkin said, pointing to a desk.

I waved my hand.

"I think I'm supposed to be in Miss Cole's room," I blurted out. Everyone looked at me.

"I don't believe so, Alice." Mrs. Plotkin checked her list. "Your name is right here."

"Well, when Dad registered me, they told him I'd have Miss Cole," I lied. I didn't even have time to be nervous.

"Perhaps he misunderstood," the teacher said. "Would you like to go to the office and check?"

With my heart pounding, I went out into the empty corridor and discovered I didn't know the way to the office. I opened the door to a broom closet, and the janitor told me which way to go.

When I got there, I felt really scared. Once you tell a lie, you have to tell another to keep it going.

"Mrs. Plotkin thinks there's been a mistake," I told the secretary. "I'm supposed to be in Miss Cole's room." I gave her my name.

"Let me see," she said. "I've got the master list right here."

I could feel my pulse pounding in my ears as she reached in her drawer and took out some papers.

"No," she said. "You're in the right room."

"Well . . . I . . . I thought when my father talked to the principal that . . . he said . . ."

"Do you want to see Mr. Edgecomb?"

I nodded. I couldn't tell which was shaking more, my teeth or my knees.

"He's with a parent. Just sit down on that bench, and he'll be through in a minute."

I couldn't believe what I was doing. I had never told a major lie in my life. I tried to remember all the people I'd known who had been transferred from one class to another and could only think of one—a boy back in fourth grade who sassed Mrs. Saunders.

He didn't exactly sass. He just repeated everything she said. If she said, "Open your geography books, please," he said, "Open your geography books, please." Day after day. She scolded, she punished, but he wouldn't stop, and so she had him transferred because of a "personality clash."

I could hear people moving around inside Mr. Edgecomb's office, preparing to leave. I wished suddenly that I had brought the Saint Agnes card under my mattress, something to hold onto. I prayed to Saint Agnes to please let me get into Miss Cole's class, and then I made the sign of the cross, except I didn't know exactly how to do it. I touched my head first and then I did it backwards, just to make sure. The secretary was watching, and I was glad when the principal came out and took me into his office.

Mr. Edgecomb looked like a rooster. He had a narrow face with red wavy hair that sort of came to a peak in the center of his head. Beneath his chin, folds of loose flesh hung down almost to his shirt collar. I couldn't understand it because he wasn't fat. I decided finally that he had once weighed five-hundred pounds and when he lost it, his skin had been permanently stretched.

"What can I do for you?" he asked and sat down behind his desk.

It was to be the third lie I had told that day: "I

thought . . . that after my father registered me . . . he said . . . you said . . . I could be in Miss Cole's classroom."

Mr. Edgecomb looked puzzled. "When was that?"

"Last week."

He got out some papers. "You're Alice McKinley?"

I nodded.

Mr. Edgecomb was speaking softly: "I don't make promises I can't keep, Alice. We let the computer decide who goes where, and it works out best that way."

"But . . . my dad wanted me to be in her classroom." I was desperate.

"If you're new to our school," he said, studying me carefully, "you wouldn't know very much about any of our teachers, would you? Why would your father want you to have Miss Cole?"

I could feel my face starting to burn. I realized now what was happening. I was definitely growing backwards. All the stupid things I was doing would get even more stupid as time went on. Embarrassing myself with Donald Sheavers was nothing compared to this. What awful thing would I do when I got to high school? To *college*, for heaven's sake?

I sat staring down at the Kleenex I held clutched in my hand. I was picking off little pieces, rolling them between my fingers, and dropping them on Mr. Edgecomb's carpet.

"We've found," the principal was saying, "that it's best not to go playing musical chairs with our classes.

We'd have pupils moving back and forth all year. We like to think that all three of our sixth-grade teachers are excellent, Alice, and I think if you just put forth the effort, you'll find that you and Mrs. Plotkin will get along fine."

I swallowed.

He leaned forward in his chair to let me know that I could leave. I bent down and picked up all the little pieces of Kleenex and then, without even looking at him, left the office and went back down the corridor.

I passed Miss Cole's room on the way. She was sitting on top of her desk with her legs crossed, and the sun came in the window behind her, like a halo around her hair. She was talking and smiling at the same time, and she looked like a goddess. Everyone was smiling back at her, worshipping her there in the sunlight.

Tears welled up in my eyes. I wanted to be in Miss Cole's classroom more than anything I'd ever wanted in my life. More than I'd wanted to be kissed by Donald Sheavers. I *needed* to be there—needed for someone to make me over. I moved on down the hall to Room 217, and there stood Mrs. Plotkin beside the American flag, her heavy legs planted firmly on the floor, her green dress sagging.

I slipped in and took the empty seat. Mrs. Plotkin was reading off some instructions from a mimeographed paper, and she moved down the aisle, put a copy on my desk, and moved back up to the flag again without missing a word. I saw some girls glance at me, then at each other and smirk, and suddenly I felt furious at the way things were working out in my life.

"And now, let's look at the vocabulary list," Mrs. Plotkin was saying.

"And now, let's look at the vocabulary list," I mimicked.

It seemed impossible that the voice was mine. It was loud enough to be heard halfway across the room. Everyone turned and stared at me. Mrs. Plotkin heard also. Out of the corner of my eye I saw the green dress pause, and I knew that she was looking right at me.

"And now," she repeated again slowly, each word soft but distinct, "let's look at the vocabulary list."

I leaned back in my chair, eyes on my lap, feeling dull and defeated. I wondered if my prayer to Saint Agnes had backfired because I wasn't Catholic. How on earth did I think that the special patroness of bodily purity would help me with my lie? Slowly the drone of Mrs. Plotkin's voice filled up the space around me, and after a while I wasn't the center of attention anymore. I wasn't anything; I couldn't feel anything. My whole body was numb.

At lunchtime, the fifth-and sixth-graders ate together in the all-purpose room. I sat down at a table with Elizabeth Price, because none of the girls in my room wanted to eat with me—not after the way I'd mimicked the teacher. Everyone was talking about their teachers and how much they liked them.

"Miss Cole's in charge of the safety patrol," a girl

named Charlene Verona was saying. "She's going to try to get us sweat shirts with 'Parkhaven School' on the back in blue letters."

"Mr. Weber says we'll be going to Chesapeake Bay for our campout," Elizabeth said happily. "We're going out on a boat."

"Have you seen Miss Cole's red sports car?" Charlene Verona went on. "Sometimes, if you stay after school to help, she'll drive you home in it."

I took a bite of the egg sandwich Dad had made for me that morning. It tasted like garbage. I was looking desperately for a way to salvage sixth grade, something to cling to so it wouldn't be a total waste.

"How do you get to be a safety patrol?" I asked Charlene.

"Oh, those were all chosen last year," she told me.

We stood out by the wall talking after lunch, watching some boys play soccer. Miss Cole was walking around the jungle gym with a cluster of girls beside her, all laughing and talking and reaching up to touch her earrings. One of them, a fourth-grader, I think, was begging to carry her purse, which just showed how much they loved her.

The afternoon moved in slow motion, and so did Mrs. Plotkin.

Mrs. *Plod*-kin, I said to myself and wrote that down on my notebook. Mrs. *Plod*-kin would never drive a red sports car because she'd never fit behind the wheel. Mrs. *Plod*-kin would never go to Chesapeake Bay, either, because she'd sink the boat. Everything she did at the front of the room was ugly and awkward.

At two-thirty, she gathered up all the math papers. She was smiling.

"In this class," she said, "we stop whatever we are doing at two-thirty and enjoy a book together. I'm going to start off this semester with a book that other classes have enjoyed—William Armstrong's *Sounder*."

I closed my eyes when she began to read to show her I wasn't the least bit interested. It was about a boy and his family and a dog. I pretended to be asleep and after a while I began to snore, very lightly. A few kids around me snickered. Mrs. Plotkin stopped reading. The room grew very quiet, and I knew she was looking at me. I opened my eyes and stared down at my desk. The reading started again.

I began scribbling things on my notebook cover. All the kids have notebooks that are scribbled up with words and drawings and things, and I wanted mine to look old and used—as if I'd been going to Parkhaven Elementary all my life.

" 'His mother always hummed when she was worried,' " Mrs. Plotkin read. " 'When she held a well child on her lap and rocked back and forth, she sang. But when she held a sick child close in her arms and the rocker moved just enough to squeak a little, she would hum. Sometimes she hummed so softly that the child heard the deep concerned breathing of terror above the sound of the humming. . . .' "

I don't know why it came to me then, but it suddenly occurred to me that Mrs. Plotkin was married. I looked up and stared. I couldn't quite believe it. Somebody loved her. Passionately. Somebody got in bed with her every night and had breakfast with her every morning.

Life is weird, I wrote on the front of my notebook, and decorated the letters with little flowers and scrolls.

The bell rang before Mrs. Plotkin had finished the chapter, and she said she would read the rest the next day. I figured that's what the Mrs. *Plod*-kins of the world had to do to keep you interested: lure you back with stories.

She hadn't assigned any homework, so I crammed my notebook into my desk, pulled out my sweater, and started for the door.

"Alice," I heard her saying, "I'd like to talk with you."

5

Hiding Out at the Melody Inn

I FROZE with one foot in the air, like I'd been playing *Mother, May I?* and forgot the "May I?"

I put my foot down slowly and turned around. Mrs. Plotkin was standing against her desk with her hands on a little plexiglass paperweight, the kind that snows when you shake it. I knew she wasn't going to say anymore until I came over. Edging closer, I stopped two rows away.

Her face seemed a little different. Pinker. I didn't know whether she was angry or embarrassed, but she definitely looked uncomfortable. That made two of us.

"All of our regular safety patrols were chosen last spring," she told me, "but Miss Cole has asked each sixth-grade teacher to select one student as a substitute. I wonder if you'd be interested?"

I couldn't believe what I was hearing. My ears burned.

"Yes," I mumbled.

"Good. Substitutes attend all the meetings of the safety patrol, and the first one is tomorrow at noon. You can bring your lunch and eat in Miss Cole's classroom."

I nodded. I couldn't think of one single thing to say, not even "I'm sorry."

Mrs. Plotkin looked down at the paperweight and turned it over and over in her hands. The snow was flying around like crazy—around a little doghouse with Snoopy on top.

"You know," she said finally, "there are many times we find ourselves in situations we don't especially like and we just have to make the best of it. Talking sometimes helps, though. Is there anything you want to tell me, Alice?"

She must have thought I was crazy. How was I supposed to tell her that I didn't want to be in her room, that I wanted Miss Cole for my adopted mother? I shook my head, feeling awful.

Mrs. Plotkin set the paperweight on her desk. The snow began to settle and covered up Snoopy.

"All right," she said. "I'll give your name to Miss Cole, and I'm sure she'll be glad to have you."

"Thanks," I said.

I walked quickly outside, my heart pounding with relief and excitement. All I could think about was how maybe I could be one of Miss Cole's girls after all. I wouldn't be rude to Mrs. Plotkin again, but I wouldn't give up trying to get in Miss Cole's classroom, either.

Elizabeth Price and the other girls had gone on

without me and I was glad, because I wanted to think about this alone. I imagined myself standing on a corner in a *Parkhaven Elementary* sweat shirt with my patrol belt across my chest. I imagined a little child stepping off the curb in front of a bread truck and me pulling her back and getting a medal. By the time I reached the corner, I was practically Miss Cole's adopted daughter, taking her soup when she was sick and sitting her cat when she went on vacation. I didn't even know if she had a cat.

"Hey! Wait a minute!"

I felt a hand grab my sleeve as I stepped off the curb just as a mail truck screeched on its brakes.

"You're not supposed to cross until I signal," the safety patrol said, and I found myself looking right into the face of the red-haired boy with the blue underpants.

I couldn't believe this was happening to me. I hadn't recognized him that morning, but now, without his hooded jacket, there was no mistake. I could tell that he recognized me too. He gave me that dazed sort of stare and then turned away and began swinging his arm without looking back. I didn't stop running until I reached our street.

I was trapped. If I went home, Elizabeth Price would be waiting to tell me all the wonderful things she was going to do in Mr. Weber's class. If I went back to the playground, I'd run into Mrs. Plotkin. I couldn't stay around on the street either. No telling where the boy with the blue underpants would turn up next. I decided to keep right on walking the four blocks to Georgia Avenue and spend the next hour at the Melody Inn.

Dad's store is on a corner. The show window facing the side street is full of tee shirts and guitars and drum sets with blue transparent heads. The show window facing Georgia Avenue has a piano in it with a violin resting on top and a pair of white gloves on top of the violin. A yellow book called *Mozart: Nineteen Sonatas for the Piano* is on the music stand.

Mostly what you see when you first walk in are clarinets and organs and violas and cymbals. There are stairs at the back of the store leading up to the loft, with the glass cubicles for lessons.

It's the low-ceilinged room under the loft that I like best, the Shoppe. The shelves are full of little boxes, each holding a certain size guitar string or pick. There are drum keys, tuning pegs, bow screws, chin-rests, and snakelike things for cleaning the spit out of trumpets. Tee shirts in all designs and colors hang from hooks on the ceiling: rock posters decorate the walls.

"Well, Alice, what are you buying today?" Loretta Jenkins always asks me. Loretta runs the Shoppe. She's got wild curly hair and she always pulls a tee shirt over whatever else she's wearing. On this day she was wearing one that said, "Brahms Does it Best."

Dad says Loretta is sort of a birdbrain, but I like her better than Janice Sherman who works over in the sheet music section. Janice wears glasses with a chain around them. I get ten percent off on anything I buy, but

I never buy sheet music because I can't even carry a tune. Whenever there's a birthday and I start to sing, people stare at me. I can tell it sounds awful, but I can't tell you why.

Once, when I was in second grade, we were practicing "The Merry Little Horses" for a PTA meeting, and the teacher stopped the music and had us sing it row by row. When she got to ours, she had us sing it two by two. When it got down to me and a girl named Margaret Keiler, the teacher asked me if, instead of singing, I might like to play the triangle. At the PTA that night, while the other children sang, I held the triangle in one hand, a stick in the other, and at the end of each verse, I went *Ping*.

Anyway, as soon as I come in the Shoppe, Loretta starts the gift wheel. It's a circular glass case that goes around and around. If you see something interesting, you can press the button and the wheel will stop.

There are music boxes with little conductors on top who wave their arms, coffee mugs with composers' names on them, plaster busts of Bach and Handel, pads of paper that say "Chopin Liszt" instead of "Shopping List," plastic rain bonnets with notes painted round the edge, and little ceramic insects playing instruments. Sometimes, if something gets chipped, Loretta lets me have it. I waited weeks for someone to drop a ceramic cricket, but nobody did.

On this particular day, however, there was something new on the gift wheel—a tortoise-shell barrette with the treble clef painted on it in gold. The minute I saw it, I thought of Miss Cole and her beautiful hair.

Loretta saw me looking at the barrette.

"Just got that in this morning," she said.

I pressed the button to make the gift wheel stop, and Loretta got it out for me and laid it on the counter. I ran my finger over the smooth finish.

"How much?" I asked her.

"Three dollars, less ten percent," she said.

I imagined walking into Miss Cole's safety patrol meeting the next day. I imagined myself going up to her afterwards and giving her the barrette. Then I imagined how she would put her arm around me and together we would go back to Mrs. Plotkin's classroom and move all the stuff out of my desk.

Loretta waited for me to make up my mind. She keeps a wad of gum stuck in one cheek to chew when my dad isn't around, and I could hear her jaws working on it. I ran my finger over the tortoise-shell barrette once more, then reached down in my jeans pocket, took out my entire allowance for the week, and laid it on the counter.

6
Looking After Lester

WE GOT PIZZA from Shakey's and took it home. Dinner is family time in our house. Dad won't let anybody watch the news or turn on the radio or bring a magazine to the table.

"You mean I have to sit here and look at her?" Lester said once. That was when I was still chewing with my mouth open.

"The way you eat, Lester, that amounts to about five and a half minutes," Dad said.

I learned to chew with my mouth closed, but that's about all the table manners I know—that and how you don't reach across someone's plate for the butter. I'm always afraid I'll get invited somewhere and they'll have two spoons or two forks at each plate and then I'll just die.

I do a lot of my dying at the table, actually. There are just too many things that can go wrong. I read some-where that if you have dinner with the queen and you make a mistake, she'll make the same mistake just so you'll feel better. It told how a man picked up his finger bowl once and drank the water, so the queen had to do it too. And another time a woman ate a paper doily that was sticking to the bottom of her tart, so the queen had to eat hers too. I decided right then that there are lots of things brought to tables that aren't meant for you to eat at all.

But the problems don't end there. I know for sure. The week after we moved here, Elizabeth Price had a birthday and her parents took some of her friends to a Chinese restaurant. We don't eat Chinese much because of the monosodium glutamate, so I just let Mrs. Price order for me. All the dishes came to the table with silver covers on them, and Mrs. Price told each of us to take some of whatever was closest and pass it on.

Everyone else found snow peas and bamboo shoots and things, but I found a stack of thin white circles about the size of handkerchiefs. I looked helplessly around the table, but everybody was exclaiming over the shrimp and chicken, so I just lifted one of the little circles out. It was warm. I decided right away it was one of those hot napkins waiters bring for you to wipe your sticky fingers, so I carefully began wiping each finger with the warm circle.

Suddenly a girl exclaimed, "Look what Alice is doing with the pancakes!"

Pancakes? I stared.

"Oooh! Yuk!" everyone screamed.

Mrs. Price tried to laugh it off. She showed me how to spread the circle out on my plate, dump some moo-shi pork in the center, bring up the edges and fold them over like a baby in a blanket. If I had sat at that table for a thousand years, I never would have guessed that this was the way you ate moo-shi pork. I had never even heard of moo-shi anything.

"Terrific day," Dad was saying now at our own table. He picked up a piece of pizza and wound the long string of cheese on top before he took a bite. "I got three more sign-ups for music lessons—two for piano and one for saxophone. I'm going to have to hire another instructor at this rate." Dad looks like Lester will probably look in thirty years except he's neater and he doesn't have as much hair.

"Had a pretty good day myself," said Lester. "Got this absolute fox for my anthropology teacher." He grinned and looked over at Dad. "Maybe I could introduce you."

Dad smiled too. "No thanks." He turned to me. "What about you, Al? First day go okay?"

I flicked a black olive off my pizza. Then I flicked off a piece of anchovy and a mushroom. Should I tell them? I wondered. Should I say that I missed out on getting the most beautiful woman in the world for my teacher, and then humiliated myself before the class? Should I say I was asked to stay after school for being sassy and then ran into the one boy in the whole world besides Donald Sheavers whom I never wanted to see again?

"It went great," I said.

"Good!" Dad smiled. "It looks as though we're all getting settled then! I'd like to see you have some friends in once in a while, Al. They're welcome any time, you know."

Simply marvelous, I thought. *Alice McKinley cordially invites Elizabeth Price, Mrs. Plotkin, and the boy in the blue underpants. I'm delirious with all the fun I'm having in Silver Spring.*

I really was excited about school the next day, though. I made a tuna fish sandwich, and then I scraped it off and put chicken slices on the bread instead. I didn't want to go in Miss Cole's room with a smelly sandwich. I put on my new Levis and a red tee shirt from the Melody Inn with Leonard Bernstein's face on it. Then I slipped the tortoise-shell barrette in my back pocket and started off.

All through social studies and math I watched the clock, waiting for the magic moment. Mrs. Plotkin smiled at me when the bell rang at noon. I smiled back, picked up my lunch, and went hurrying across the hall to Miss Cole's room.

She had placed the chairs in a circle, and we all ate with our lunch on our laps. Miss Cole introduced us, the regulars first and then the substitutes. When the red-haired boy was introduced, I could feel a blush spreading across my face. Knowing that his name was Patrick made it worse. It was like knowing that his underwear was "Fruit of the Loom" or something.

After the introductions, Miss Cole passed around some cookies she had made herself.

"They're kamikaze cookies, because they're suicide on your teeth." She laughed.

They were the most delicious things I had ever tasted—little heaps of peanuts, chow mein noodles, and melted chocolate. I tried to imagine Mrs. Plotkin making cookies like that. If Mrs. Plotkin made cookies, they'd be oatmeal.

When Miss Cole moved, her legs sort of swung from the hips. When she ate, her beautiful white teeth sank delicately down in her sandwich. Even when she swallowed, it was never a gulp. Her beautiful long throat just seemed to ripple. I tried holding my sandwich exactly the way she held hers. She crossed her ankles, I crossed mine. I even tried to get my cheeks to dimple, and kept putting my finger up to check.

"I'VE ORDERED some sweat shirts for us," she announced, "and each of you will get one. I want all of you to look really sharp on your posts this year."

I beamed with pleasure.

We watched a short film about the seven most dangerous things children can do in traffic and what to watch out for when it rains. I loved being in Miss Cole's classroom, smelling her perfume and listening to the little clink of her bracelets. I could have sat there forever, but when the film was over, so was the meeting.

Patrick put the projector away, so I began straightening the chairs, going as slow as I could so that everyone else would leave before me. Finally, there I was, alone with Miss Cole.

"Oh, don't bother with those chairs," she told me, turning toward the window. She closed her eyes and smiled at the sun on her face. "Go out and enjoy this beautiful weather while you can. There are only five minutes left of the lunch period."

I reached down in the pocket of my jeans.

"I . . . I wanted to give you something," I said, and took out a folded tissue.

"It's clean," I told her, so she wouldn't think I'd used it. Out fell the barrette. "It's for your hair," I said, handing it to her. "I saw it in my dad's store and thought you might like it."

Miss Cole didn't seem to know what to say. Her green eyes opened a little wider and her forehead sort of buckled into a frown, but she was smiling. She was trying to smile, anyway. "Well . . !" she said finally. "This is a clef sign, isn't it? What kind of store does your father have?"

"The Melody Inn. He's the manager," I told her, and my voice was shaky with excitement. I kept wanting her to put it in her hair, but she just stood holding it in the palm of one hand.

"It's lovely, Alice," she said. "I don't wear barrettes much, but . . . I think it might be just the thing to keep the hair out of my eyes when I play tennis on Saturdays. I will certainly think of you each time I wear it."

"I thought you might like it," I said again. Whenever I can't think of anything to say, I repeat myself.

I went back out to the playground happy, and turned my face up to the sun, just like Miss Cole.

There were only two things that afternoon that I hated: going back to Mrs. Plotkin's class and passing Patrick on the way home. Patrick and I have this system, though: when I look at him, he turns away; when he looks at me, I turn away. I know if I ever tried to say anything at all to him, it would be something dumb like, "How are your Fruit-of-the-Looms this morning?"

When I got home, my brother's car was parked out front. I went inside, and back to the kitchen to feel around under the bread for the potato chips. Lester always hides the things he likes. After I found those I looked under the lettuce in the refrigerator for the dip. Once you know Lester's system, you can find almost anything. I had just started down to the family room with my snack when I heard a girl's voice from upstairs. I stopped there in the hallway. The sound came again, the sound of a girl laughing in Lester's room.

Something told me that Lester wasn't supposed to have a girl in his room. Not with the door closed, anyway. Not when Dad wasn't home.

I thought of knocking on his door and asking for help with my homework. I thought about pounding on his door and yelling "Fire!" Then I thought of something else.

I took the potato chips and dip to the top of the stairs and began eating as loudly as I could just outside Lester's door. I tried eating two chips at a time with my mouth open, then three, then propping them sideways between my teeth. I practiced mouthing all the vowels while I was chewing to see which one was loudest. Chewing makes the most noise when your lips are open in the shape of an "i" or an "e," if anybody wants to know. After each swallow, I smacked my lips as hard as I could and slurrrrrrped the dip off each potato chip.

Lester's door flew open.

"Just what the heck do you think you're doing?"

I held out the chips. "Want some?"

"Drop dead."

I slurped again.

"Beat it, Al," he told me.

"It's a free country."

"*Beat* it!"

"I have as much right here as you do," I said. I was being so bratty I could hardly stand myself. I just didn't know what to do about Lester and that girl in his room.

Suddenly Lester's door opened wider and the girl came out. She had long straight brown hair and pink-tinted glasses. She was holding Lester's high school yearbook.

"Maybe we should go downstairs, Les," she told

him, and she smiled at me as she stepped over my legs to pass. I thought she was kind of nice.

I knew that Lester could have stepped on my legs and broken them in three places, but he just glared down at me and followed the girl over to the couch where she opened the yearbook again.

"I'm Marilyn Rawley," the girl said to me.

"Delighted to meet you. I'm Alice McKinley," I answered in my very best company voice. I had rescued the girl and saved Lester's reputation. Mother, if I had a mother, would have been proud.

That night I took out the poster from behind my dresser and added a few more things. In the "Forward" column I wrote that I no longer chewed with my mouth open, that I had given Miss Cole a present she liked, and that I had learned to get girls out of Lester's room. In the "Backward" column I had to write about how I had wiped my fingers with moo-shi pork pancakes and how I had treated Mrs. Plotkin. The columns were exactly even; I was just marking time.

7
The Maharaja's Magic

THREE WEEKS after school started, I was standing on the steps at recess watching the fourth graders jump rope. Charlene Verona was showing us her new designer jeans with a horseshoe on the back pocket.

"Miss Cole says she has a pair exactly like mine," Charlene said proudly. "When we have our class picnic, she's going to wear hers, and we'll be twins."

I was so jealous of Charlene at that moment I could hardly breathe. My lips were smiling, but my teeth were clamped together so hard that the fillings hurt.

"Miss Cole is *so* much fun!" Charlene went on. "She even let me use her nail polish yesterday after school."

I choked.

Elizabeth Price was not to be outdone, however. "I'm really glad *I* got a *man* for a teacher this year," she said. "He treats us like we're grown up. Sometimes he even calls us 'Miss' and 'Mr.' 'Miss Price, would you care to put the third problem on the blackboard?' he'll say. I heard he plays the guitar, and when you go on the overnight, everybody sings."

Right away I fantasied everyone singing around a bonfire while Mr. Weber played his guitar, with me standing in the back with a triangle going *ping*.

And then I realized that both girls were looking at me.

"It's too bad you got Mrs. Plotkin," said Elizabeth.

The only thing I hated more than being in Mrs. Plotkin's room was being pitied, and I simply was not going to let that happen. I laughed my "Miss Cole" laugh and sort of tossed my hair.

"Oh, it's not as bad as you think," I said gaily. "Mrs. Plotkin is *so* nice, and every day, no matter what we're doing, she stops at two thirty and reads us part of a book."

I knew that didn't sound like much compared to matching designer jeans and singing around a bonfire. The girls were looking at me strangely, and I went on: "If I could choose any class I wanted, I just might stay right where I am."

I could see they didn't quite believe me. In fact, they weren't even looking at me any longer, they were looking somewhere behind me, and I turned to see Mrs. Plotkin standing just inside the door. She smiled as she came out on the steps, holding a plant she was setting out to sun.

"What a nice thing to say, Alice!" she said. "And if I could choose any girl in the whole school to be in my room, I just might put Alice McKinley at the head of the list."

I gave Mrs. Plotkin a weak smile, and she edged on down the steps with her potted geranium. The terrible, awful truth was that now I had boxed myself into a corner. Even if Miss Cole *asked* me to be in her class, how could I switch?

The next day I tried not to look at Mrs. Plotkin at all. Every time I thought her eyes were on me, I looked away. I was the first one out the door after school. The day after that went the same. I couldn't go not looking at her forever, though. I was already not looking at Patrick, and the crazy thing about not looking at somebody is that you are always looking at them to see if they're not looking at you.

I lived for Wednesdays, when the patrols ate in Miss Cole's room. I thought there was nothing in the world so wonderful as the perfume Miss Cole wore on her shoulders. When you walked in Mrs. Plotkin's room, you smelled lunch sacks—bananas and baloney sandwiches. You smelled chalk and raincoats and library paste. But when you walked in Miss Cole's room, you smelled gardenias or something. I mean, just standing in Miss Cole's doorway said that you were somewhere special.

It was on a Wednesday, when I got home from school, that I opened an envelope marked "Occupant." I almost never get any mail. Lester gets things from the junior college, and Dad gets all the bills. Everything addressed to Occupant, they leave on the coffee table for me. Once I got a bar of free soap. Another time I got a packet of Tang and a free leaf bag. This time, it was a purple card in cellophane that said, *Maharaja's Magic—the only perfume you will ever need.*

I ripped open the cellophane and pulled the card out. The perfume was really strong. I figured they must have dipped the card in *Maharaja's Magic* and then let it dry overnight. I took it upstairs and stuck it in the drawer with my tee shirts so they would smell good when I went to school the next day.

On Thursday I put on my George Gershwin tee shirt and my Niagara Falls tee shirt over that.

"Whew!" said Lester, when I sat down at the table. "What smells?"

"Your feet, probably," I told him. Lester wouldn't know gardenias from garbage.

Around nine, as I approached the school, Elizabeth Price said, "Someone's wearing *perfume!*"

"It's me," I said, before I realized it was no compliment. "It's *Maharaja's Magic.*"

"It's so strong!" said Elizabeth, making a face. "You must have used a whole bottle."

I should have gone home right then and changed. I should have taken a shower and hung all my tee shirts out to air. Instead, I walked on into the classroom.

The girl who sits behind me is almost as pretty as Elizabeth Price. Her name is Pamela Jones, and until this particular morning, I thought she was my friend.

"What stinks?" said Pamela.

I didn't even have time to answer before somebody else said, "Euuyuk!"

One of the boys went over to the window and stuck his head out like he was going to be sick, and then all the boys started acting dumb. They'd take a couple steps toward me, then grab their throats and gag. The girls were giggling. I sat down at my desk and pretended I didn't notice. Mrs. Plotkin noticed, though. I could tell she was watching.

"What happened?" Pamela whispered behind me. "Did you spill something on your clothes?"

I didn't even answer.

It was probably the very worst day of my life. I couldn't go home and change at noon because then everyone would know how embarrassed I was. I played soccer instead, in hopes that all that running around would air the tee shirts out. What it did was mix some sweat with *Maharaja's Magic* so that, when I came in after lunch, I smelled like the Maharaja's horse. I wanted to disappear. Mrs. Plotkin had opened a window, but the breeze just blew the perfume off me and carried it around the room.

When the bell rang at three and all the kids started for the door, I hung back. I wanted to wait until all the girls had left so I could walk home alone. I spilled my box of colored pencils on the floor on purpose and then slowly picked them up, one by one.

"Alice," said Mrs. Plotkin when the others had gone, "I wonder if you'd be interested in helping me out occasionally after school—when you're not on patrol duty, of course."

I was so grateful for an excuse to stay that I would have even cleaned the gerbil cage.

"Sure," I told her.

She said that her plants needed watering and the blackboard needed cleaning and that sometime, if I really felt like staying longer, I could rearrange the supply cupboard. I started in on the plants, then scrubbed the blackboard, and when I was pretty sure that the other girls were home, I left.

I threw the Maharaja in the garbage can and put all my tee shirts in the wash. *Wore perfume to school,* I had to write on my poster, under the "Backward" column. Then I sat out on the steps and wondered what I would be like when I was twenty. Most of the girls who were getting married and had their pictures in the paper were twenty. It told where they had gone to school and where they worked and how they were the granddaughters of the late Admiral and Mrs. Barker or somebody, and how the bride wore a gown with a scalloped neckline and tiny seed pearls. I figured that any granddaughter of a late admiral who knew about scalloped necklines was beyond doing stupid things. When *I* was twenty, if I kept on growing backward, I would be such an embarrassment to my family that Dad would have to put me away.

The next day in English, Mrs. Plotkin announced that each year she asked her sixth graders to keep a journal. She said that journals were different from diaries because they weren't records of what happened to us so much as they were records of what we thought and felt about the things that happened. She said we were to start our journals right away, in black and white bound notebooks with lines, and turn them in at the end of May. We could write in them as often as we liked and say anything we wanted, but if we wrote something private, we should fasten those pages together with paper clips and she wouldn't read them.

"I'll bet!" said Lester at the table that night. "She probably reads those pages aloud in the teachers' lounge."

Somehow, I didn't think so. I found an old black and white notebook I'd started in third grade with only two pages used, which I carefully pulled out. Then I took my ballpoint pen with *Melody Inn* printed on one side and carefully wrote, "The Agony of Alice, page 1."

8
Bringing Up the Rear

I DECIDED that if I was ever going to get Miss Cole to sort of take me on, I had to do something more than give her little presents wrapped in Kleenex and smear myself with perfume samples. So I opened my journal with an advertisement that I hoped Mrs. Plotkin would show the other teachers:

> WANTED: Adopted Mother
> Must be tall, smart, and beautiful
> with the initials M—— C——
> SALARY: love forever

I figured that Miss Cole would know right away I was writing about her, and fantasied how her eyes would grow misty and she'd call me into her room and ask how would I like to spend Thanksgiving with her and did I need any help with Christmas shopping.

When I started on the second page, though, I knew that this was the page I would paperclip, because I wrote down all the ridiculous things I had done that I wouldn't have done if I'd had a mother. It took weeks to write all the details, the horrible humiliations, but I put down everything: Donald Sheavers, Patrick in his blue underwear, the *Maharaja's Magic*, and what happened on Halloween. *Especially* what happened on Halloween.

Parkhaven School always had a parade before their big Halloween party. Pamela Jones told me all about it while we were washing out paint brushes after art class. Pamela had just finished a six-foot mural to hang in the hall outside our door. It showed all the things you could do in autumn—apple picking, nut gathering, cider making, leaf raking—painted in red and rust and bronze and gold. I had drawn an 8½ x 11 picture of a pumpkin.

"Everyone comes to school in costume," Pamela told me, "even the principal." Pamela has long yellow hair that has never been cut. It hangs all the way down her back, and she sits on it.

I stuck a brush under the running water and ran my thumb over the bristles the wrong way. Orange paint splattered my shirt. Pamela finished the brushes while I tried to clean myself off with a paper towel.

"What are you going to wear?" I asked her.

"I've got a fantastic costume from my dance recital," Pamela said. "It's a horse, and it comes in two parts. You want to wear it with me?"

I knew right away which part of the horse Pamela wanted me to be, but it didn't matter. I didn't have any ideas of my own, and when I'd asked Lester about it he said, "Just go to school without combing your hair. You can't get more gruesome than that."

"Sure," I told Pamela.

For a week before Halloween, that's all the girls talked about. Elizabeth Price's mother was making her a gypsy costume. She'd been working on it since September, Elizabeth told me. The skirt had three ruffles around the bottom in purple, pink, and green, the blouse was red, and there was a purple satin vest with sequins on it. Elizabeth even had her ears pierced so she could wear some hoop earrings.

Charlene Verona was going to come to the parade as a bottle of Heinz catsup. She said that her father had built the frame over the summer, and her sister had painted it for her. I swallowed. The nice thing about being a horse's rear end, I decided, was that no one would know who I was.

The day of the party, Dad said he would walk over to the school around one to watch our parade. I told him he didn't really have to, but Dad always tries to do what he thinks Momma would do if she were alive. The past five years he even thought up a costume for me. In first grade I was Beethoven, in second grade I was Brahms, in third, fourth, and fifth I was Schubert, Bach, and Mozart. Every year I wore the top of Dad's old tuxedo and carried a baton. The kids thought I was trying to be a magician. That's why I didn't mind being a horse this time.

When classes let out at noon, most of the kids went home to change. I was practically the only one eating lunch in the all-purpose room. I stood at the front entrance and watched as people returned in their costumes. Mrs. Plotkin was dressed as a farmer. She had on a checked shirt, a kerchief, and an enormous pair of overalls. Two boys came as a pair of dice. Someone else was a box of Rice Krispies, and there was even a girl dressed as a television set. I saw the principal in a cowboy costume, and Mr. Weber dressed as a vampire, with fangs on either side of his mouth. But it was Miss Cole I was waiting for, and at last I saw her coming out of the teachers' lounge.

She was the most gorgeous sight I had ever seen. She was wearing a green and yellow kimono with a wide silk sash around her waist, white stockings, and little green slippers. Her hair was swept up on top of her head and held in place with a huge spray of carnations.

I couldn't take my eyes off her. Even when Patrick went by in a Superman cape, with blue tights and his blue underwear on top of them, right out there in public, I hardly even looked at him. I wanted Miss Cole for my adopted mother more than I wanted anything else in the world. I wanted her to dress me in a green and yellow kimono and show me how to wear flowers in my hair. I wanted someone to make a fuss over me and teach me how to walk in tiny little steps and bow the way Miss Cole was bowing to some of her students.

"Come on," someone said, pulling my arm, and I

turned as Pamela Jones and her mother came through the entrance holding the horse costume. I followed them to the girls' restroom. Pamela had on brown tights and tap shoes. She kept tap dancing all around the tiled floor.

Mrs. Jones smiled at me as she held out the second half of the costume, and I put my feet inside. I had to pull it up high so the legs wouldn't wrinkle.

She laughed. "You girls are going to be a riot!" The wide top was shoulder high and had snaps around it. Holding on with both hands, I stood side by side with Pamela. We looked in the mirror and laughed. Maybe it wouldn't be so bad after all, I thought. If I couldn't wear a green and yellow kimono, it was better to be a horse's rear end than it was to be some old composer that nobody knew.

Mrs. Jones kept watch at the door, and when she saw our class lining up in the hallway, she put the horse's head over Pamela. Then I bent over and put my hands on Pamela's waist, and Mrs. Jones snapped the two parts of the costume together.

"Have fun," she said.

Gingerly, I followed Pamela out into the hall. I could hear the other kids laughing as we came. Pamela's tap shoes clicked on the corridor like hoofs, and when we got up to where I figured Mrs. Plotkin was standing, Pamela did a little tap dance while I sort of weaved around behind her and tried to hang on.

"Good heavens!" said Mrs. Plotkin, laughing. "I hope whoever is behind you has enough air."

"It's Alice," said Pamela. "She's fine."

I was fine except that I couldn't see a thing but a small patch of floor beneath my face.

The parade began to move, and I followed Pamela outside, up the sidewalk toward the street.

"Oh, look at the horse!" I heard people exclaim when we passed, and Pamela would break into her tap-dance routine while I hung on for dear life.

And then a funny thing happened. I started a little routine of my own. The fancier Pamela's dancing got up front, the sillier I acted behind. Every time we came to a corner, we'd all wait while teachers scurried by on either side to stop traffic. Pamela would tap around in a circle, and I'd stand still scratching one hind leg with the other. At the next corner while Pamela did her *shuffle-step, shuffle-step, tap heel,* I'd stand with my toes pointed in, my knees bent, bouncing up and down in time with the rhythm. And when she did her Spanish number, I'd wriggle my bottom down lower and lower until I was almost sitting on the ground. People were laughing loudly, and it sounded good.

"What are you doing back there, Alice?" Pamela asked me.

"Just having fun," I told her. I pretended I was in a Conga line. I'd take three steps and kick out my left leg. Then three steps and kick out my right.

The parade had turned around and was heading back to the school. I heard my dad's chuckle when we passed where he was standing, and I decided to give the last two blocks everything I had. As we approached the next corner, I broke into my Conga step again, kicking as high as I possibly could. *One . . . two . . . three*, left leg; *one . . . two . . . three*, right. . . .

My foot made contact with something soft.

"Ouch!" a voice cried out in pain.

I knew that voice immediately, and my knees almost buckled. Skidding to a stop, I pulled at the snaps on my costume and stood up. Miss Cole was standing there rubbing her arm, her eyes smarting with the pain.

"Alice!" she said. "Why . . .?"

I tried to speak, but couldn't. There was no excuse except that I liked the way people were laughing at us; I liked acting silly. Miss Cole turned and moved swiftly on down the line, her lips pressed tightly together. My father was looking at me from up the sidewalk.

"What's happening?" Pamela kept saying.

I couldn't possibly go on. I stepped out of my half of the costume and handed it to Pamela. Then I crossed the street and started home. Dad came running over.

"Al?" he said. "Where you going?"

I didn't answer. He walked along beside me.

"I saw what happened," he said. "You should have explained to the teacher. She would have understood."

I wasn't worried about Miss Cole understanding, though. What I wanted was for her to *like* me, to *love* me, even, and I had to go kick her in the arm.

Dad went back to work at the Melody Inn, and I went up to my room and spent the rest of the day with a pillow over my face.

If I had a mother, I wrote in my journal that night, *I would have been a gypsy or a ballerina and none of this would have happened.*

9
Dinner With Marilyn

IT WAS OBVIOUS that Miss Cole wasn't going to invite me home for Thanksgiving. She had a big bruise on her arm to remember me by, for one thing. I was afraid she might not even let me in her room. She did, though, and when I explained what had happened, she just said I could have kicked some little kid in the teeth and I ought to be more careful. She talked to me and everything at patrol meetings, but her eyes didn't seem to smile at me the way they smiled at the others. And once, when someone was teasing me, Miss Cole said jokingly, "Better watch out for Alice. She kicks."

I worked twice as hard to make it up to her. I was as helpful as I could be at our weekly patrol meetings, but I didn't get to go on duty much. Once Patrick went to a concert with his parents and I got to take his corner, and another time a patrol in Mr. Weber's class threw up. But most afternoons, if I didn't feel like walking home with Elizabeth Price and Charlene, I'd stick around Mrs. Plotkin's room. Once, just before Thanksgiving, I stayed till four o'clock and straightened her supply cupboard. I threw out an old jar of dried-up paste and poured two bottles of glue together. I divided all the construction paper into separate colors, sharpened the pencils, washed the shelves, and didn't stop until the whole cupboard was clean.

"Alice, I do believe this is the best this has ever looked," Mrs. Plotkin said.

I beamed.

She was wearing a blue dress with a white collar, and I liked her in blue because it matched her eyes.

"I found a place for everything except this brown and orange paper that's faded along one edge," I told her. "I didn't know if you wanted it mixed in with the rest or not."

"Probably not," Mrs. Plotkin said. "If you want it, it's yours."

I rolled up the paper and slipped a rubber band around it.

"I hope you're going to do something nice on Thanksgiving," she said, as I put on my coat.

"We usually go to a restaurant," I told her. "My dad can't roast a turkey."

Mrs. Plotkin laughed. "Well, believe it or not, Alice, you can get through life without ever learning to roast one. Have a good time."

"You too," I said. All the way home, though, I wondered where Mrs. Plotkin was going to celebrate

Thanksgiving. I hadn't asked her. Maybe her husband was dead and she didn't have any cousins or anything. Maybe she was going to spend Thanksgiving sitting in front of the TV with a Morton's frozen dinner on her lap.

When I got home, I cut the brown and orange paper into strips, made a huge chain, and strung it around the whole living room—over the lamps, the doorway, and the back of the sofa.

"What's this for?" Lester asked.

"Thanksgiving," I told him. "Don't you know *any-thing?*"

Dad invited Janice Sherman from the Melody Inn to come to the restaurant with us for Thanksgiving because she's single, and then he had to invite Loretta Jenkins, the birdbrain, because she's single, too. Lester said it was the worst decision Dad ever made. Loretta's a vegetarian and she kept stealing vegetables off Lester's plate to fill her up.

"What's that?" she said. "A water chestnut? I *love* water chestnuts." And she'd poke at it with her fork. "What's that? A mushroom? I *love* mushrooms." She'd wave her fork again at Lester.

I like Loretta better than Janice, though. Janice is the one in the sheet music department who wears her glasses on a chain. I think she's been in sheet music too long.

When we sat down at the table and Janice saw the

bouquet of flowers in the middle, she said, "What a symphony of color!"

When the shrimp cocktails arrived, Janice said, "What a lovely overture to a meal!"

When the pumpkin pie was served, she clasped her hands and said, "The grand finale!"

"You know what, Dad?" Lester said when we'd taken them both back home. "You work with a couple of airheads."

I wondered about Mrs. Plotkin again and whether she would have come with us if I'd asked. I'll bet Lester would have liked her better than Janice or Loretta.

I told Dad it was a great Thanksgiving, though, because he was leaving the next morning for a three-day convention in New York. I went up in his room to help him pack.

"What was Thanksgiving like when Momma was alive?" I asked, as I polished his shoes with an undershirt and put them in his bag.

"Well, we always spent it with your Aunt Sally and Uncle Milt. We'd pack your high chair in the car, and your mother would feed you strained beets while the rest of us ate turkey."

I remembered watching a baby eat zweiback once in a restaurant, and it was disgusting.

"I'll bet I was a mess," I said.

"Yes, particularly when you got to the strained spinach," Dad told me, and laughed.

The thing about mothers, I was thinking, is that

they like you regardless, no matter how repulsive you are. No matter how many stupid things you do. The thing about mothers, in fact, is that they keep you from doing a lot of dumb things in the first place. I couldn't imagine Elizabeth Price or Charlene Verona doing some of the stupid things I had done. It didn't seem fair that Charlene, who had a mother, also had Miss Cole for a teacher and got to use her nail polish.

Dad left money so Lester and I could go to the Hot Shoppe the next night for dinner, but Lester's girl friend came over instead to cook for us.

She was wearing a long skirt and a blouse with puffy sleeves and she looked absolutely beautiful, almost as pretty as Miss Cole. Lester had on jeans and an old sweat shirt and was walking around in his stocking feet.

Marilyn had brought a wok with her. She showed me how to make stir-fried chicken and vegetables. It seemed as though she was unusually nice to me that night. We talked about all kinds of things, like how long it takes to get used to panty hose and how to take care of your cuticles. I didn't even know I *had* cuticles. I set the table and sliced the bread she'd made, and just before dinner, I went upstairs and put on my long blue night-gown and my best blouse over the top, so I'd look like Marilyn. If Lester married her, I realized, she'd be my sister-in-law, and I wouldn't even need Miss Cole.

"What the heck have *you* got on?" Lester said when I sat down.

"I think she looks lovely," said Marilyn. "At least she's wearing shoes."

Lester got up, slipped on his loafers, and came back to the table.

I did everything Marilyn did. I spread my napkin over my lap, ate little tiny bites like she did, and rested my arms, not my elbows, on the table. When Lester made a joke, I even laughed delicately and tipped my head to one side. Lester looked at me strangely.

Something was wrong, though, between Lester and Marilyn. Halfway through dinner, I could just tell. When Marilyn talked to me, she smiled, but when she talked to Lester, she looked sort of sad. Lester guessed something was wrong too, and the quieter Marilyn got, the more jokes he made; but it got to the place where I was the only one who was laughing. Finally I realized that Marilyn had come over to cook our dinner because she was going to break up with Lester and she was trying to make it easy on him. I couldn't stand it anymore. I said I'd do the dishes and went out in the kitchen and closed the door, but now and then I still heard their voices.

"We're too different, Lester," Marilyn said. "It just wouldn't work."

Lester was saying something to her, but I couldn't make out what. His voice was soft and urgent, the way he talks to Dad when he needs the car. And finally Marilyn's voice again:

"I'm sorry, Les, but I just want out."

A few minutes later Marilyn stuck her head in the kitchen to say goodnight to me, and then she left. I heard the sound of her car starting up, and then Lester went up to his room.

I sat down at the kitchen table with my head in my hands. I wasn't the only one who missed having a mother. If Momma were here right now, I bet she'd have gone up to Lester and said something nice. I thought of all the awful things I'd said to him in my lifetime and felt even worse. Finally I got up, took a Sprite from the refrigerator and a plate of gingersnaps, and went up to Lester's room.

I opened his door just a crack.

"Can I come in?" I asked. He didn't answer, so I went in. He was lying on his back on the bed, staring up at the ceiling. I softly crossed the room and set the Sprite and cookies beside his bed.

"I just wanted to make you feel better," I said. "I'm sorry about Marilyn."

Lester looked at me and then stared at the ceiling some more.

"Thanks," he said finally.

I sat down on the floor with my back against the wall and stayed there for a long time without saying anything. Lester didn't even seem to know I was there. Now and then he'd sigh, a lonely sigh.

"I miss her, too," I said finally.

Lester jumped when he heard me, and then he sat up. "You still here?"

"Yeah," I said. "I was thinking about Momma. I miss her, too."

"Well, I was thinking about Marilyn," he said, and lay back down.

"You want me to stay and talk?" I asked, and when he didn't answer, I said, "There are other fish in the ocean." I'd read that somewhere; it's what you say to somebody when they lose a sweetheart. Lester still didn't answer, so I said, "Someday you'll look back on this and laugh." I'd read that, too.

Lester wasn't laughing, however. I started to say, *It's always darkest before the light*, but I didn't. I changed the subject. "What was Momma like?" I asked him. "I can't remember."

Lester put his hands behind his head. His voice was flat, but at least he was talking. "Well, she was tall, taller than Dad. She wore slacks a lot, I remember that. Long legs. Reddish-blond hair. Freckles on her arms. She used to sing songs from musicals—from *Showboat*—that was her favorite. Used to sing when she did the ironing."

I tried to imagine this mother, but somehow she didn't seem to have anything to do with me. She was tall, and I'm only average. I don't have any freckles at all, and I can't carry a tune, either.

I thought again about Marilyn and how nice she would have been as my sister-in-law.

"I'm sorry about Marilyn, Lester, I really am," I told him.

"So am I," he said, and smiled a little bit. Then he

reached for the Sprite, and I realized that we had had an entire conversation without being rude to each other once.

I got out the poster that night to bring my life up to date. I had been writing in my journal regularly, but I hadn't wanted to see how long my "Backward" list was getting. Before I could lose my nerve, I picked up the pencil and wrote, "Kicked Miss Cole," in the right-hand column. Then, under the "Forward" list, I wrote:

> Cleaned Mrs. Plotkin's cupboard
> Was Polite to Marilyn
> Was kind to Lester

For the first time, the "Forward" column was ahead.

On December first, Mrs. Plotkin collected our journals to see how we were doing. All but a few pages of mine were paper-clipped together. I didn't want her to read about Donald Sheavers. I didn't want her to know about my seeing Patrick in his underwear at The Gap, either. I certainly didn't want her to read about how disappointed I was that I didn't get Miss Cole for a teacher. The only other things I let her read were about how upset my father got when I confused memories of Momma with Aunt Sally, how I felt about Marilyn breaking up with Lester, and what happened on Halloween.

We had to read fifteen pages in our social studies books that afternoon, and while we were reading, Mrs.

Plotkin checked through our journals. I kept lifting my eyes to see when she got to mine. All the journals looked alike on the outside, but mine was the only one with paper clips holding the pages together.

Mrs. Plotkin picked it up at last. She skipped over the paper-clipped pages and read the others slowly, taking her time. I squirmed. I was glad when she went on to someone else's journal.

At two-thirty, Mrs. Plotkin read to us aloud. She had finished *Sounder* and a book called *The Incredible Journey*, and just before Thanksgiving had started *Watership Down*. We were already on chapter five:

" 'It was getting on toward moonset when they left the fields and entered the wood. Straggling, catching up with one another, keeping more or less together, they had wandered over half a mile down the fields, always following the course of the brook. . . .' "

No matter what happened to me during the day, the half hour at the end, when Mrs. Plotkin read to us, helped make up for it. When she read, her voice made pictures of the words. She read with such expression that we knew instantly what a character was feeling. The first week I was in her class, I had pretended I was doing my homework all the while she was reading. She never said anything, never paused in icy silence the way some teachers would have done. She simply read, and let the words lure me to the story. It seemed to me now impossible that I could have been so rude. It also seemed a shame that someone as kind as Mrs. Plotkin had to be so homely. *Life is unfair*, I scribbled on my desk top.

As usual, when the bell rang at three, the whole class groaned in dismay that the story was interrupted. But Mrs. Plotkin smiled as she closed the book. "We'll hear some more tomorrow," she promised. Then she handed back our journals.

I stood at my desk for a moment, thumbing through the pages to see if all the paper clips were still there. And suddenly my eye caught something that Mrs. Plotkin had written in the margin. It was on the page about Marilyn breaking up with Lester, and how we both missed having a mother.

Alice McKinley, you have a gift for words! Mrs. Plotkin had said. *Thank you for sharing that gift with me.*

I stared down at the paper, then up at Mrs. Plotkin. She was smiling. I closed my journal and smiled back, then walked quickly out the door and home, too embarrassed to stay. It was the first time in my life that I had felt embarrassed and happy, both at the same time.

10

The Bramble Bush, With Branches Thick

I WAS BEGINNING to feel a little bit special. When Charlene Verona told me how Miss Cole had let her try on her sling-back pumps, and Elizabeth showed me the whistle Mr. Weber had made for her out of a piece of bamboo, it didn't sound like much to say, "Mrs. *Plotkin* likes my journal!" so I didn't. I just kept it to myself while Charlene and Elizabeth tried to outdo each other:

"Miss Cole wears Cinnamon Coral lipstick," Charlene would say.

"Mr. Weber has a sailboat. He said if the weather's good, he'll take us out on it on the overnight," Elizabeth would say right back.

"Miss Cole's got a tape player in her sports car, and she let me hear it over the lunch hour."

"Mr. Weber's writing a song about our school, and he's going to play it for us on his guitar."

After they'd gone on for about five minutes or so,

they'd look at me to see if I was going to bawl or anything, but I didn't.

I guess this was the first time I had ever felt close to a teacher. I know that cleaning Mrs. Plotkin's blackboard wasn't much compared to wearing Miss Cole's sling-back pumps or listening to music in her sports car, but it was better than anything I'd had before, and I couldn't believe how much I looked forward to it.

Every day after school, as soon as the bell rang, I'd put some water in a bucket and start washing the blackboard. If Mrs. Plotkin was grading tests or making out her attendance report, I'd work quietly without bothering her, and she'd just smile at me when I left. It was the kind of smile you could take home with you and keep overnight. But if she was ordering supplies or checking spelling papers, we'd talk while she was working.

"How about thumbtacks, Alice?" she'd say. "Do we have enough of those?" and then I'd go look.

Sometimes we'd talk about all the different places we'd lived. I told her how I used to eat strained beets at my Aunt Sally's when we lived in Chicago, and she told me how she and her husband had lived in Missouri, Wisconsin, Louisiana, and Maryland. Then we'd find those states on her big globe. It was sort of nice to think that the very years I was living in Illinois, Mrs. Plotkin was right next door in Wisconsin.

Of all the jobs, I liked dusting the best. I especially liked dusting the globe. It was an old globe, as big as a beach ball, and there were raised places for the mountains and dents for the valleys, and sometimes I'd take a Q-tip and clean out the valleys really good. The globe was so old, though, that it was cracking, and not just along the seam; there was a jagged line all the way from Alaska to the tip of South America. Sometimes, at the end of a school year, teachers give away stuff that's old and cracked. I was given some old green chalk once, and a history book with the cover missing. I began to hope that Mrs. Plotkin would give me her old globe. I even knew where I would set it on my dresser.

By early December, I found myself wishing I wouldn't be called for patrol duty at all so I could help Mrs. Plotkin every day. And then something happened. Pamela Jones moved in on my territory.

I knew that Pamela didn't like me much after the way I had walked out on her at the Halloween parade, and I guess she decided that if anyone was going to be special in Mrs. Plotkin's class it was Pamela Jones. Because the next thing I knew, Pamela was racing to fill the bucket before I got there after school. If I reached the bucket first, Pamela would find some corner of the blackboard I'd missed and scrub it hard. If I watered the plants, she'd come along behind me with a paper towel for any drops I happened to spill. When she started rearranging the supply cupboard that I had worked so hard to clean, however, I wanted the earth to open and swallow her up.

"There's plenty of work for both of you," Mrs. Plotkin would say, and think up extra things to do. But that wasn't the point at all. I wanted Mrs. Plotkin to myself. I wanted that hour or so each day to be our own special time. I liked our talks, about where we used to live and everything. Pamela was ruining it all.

One day when she was dusting, Pamela said, "Mrs. Plotkin, did you know there's a crack in the globe?"

"Yes, dear," Mrs. Plotkin said. "That globe was always one of my favorites, but it's very old and I'm just hoping it will hold up until June."

"I *love* globes," Pamela sighed. "I always wanted one of my own. I *love* learning about other countries and people and mountains and things."

My throat felt so tight I thought I was going to choke.

"Well, someday I hope you'll have a chance to do some traveling and actually visit other places," Mrs. Plotkin answered.

She had made no promise about the globe, but Pamela had put in her bid, and I was so angry it made me dizzy. I glared at Pamela, but she just gave me a haughty smile and patted the globe as if it were hers already.

It was getting close to the holidays and the annual school pageant. Mrs. Plotkin said that every year the three sixth grades put on a play for the primary classes and that she was going to direct it. Suddenly I got this wild hope that maybe she would pick me for a leading role.

A list of characters went up on the bulletin board

outside our classroom, and sixth-graders were supposed to sign up for the parts they wanted. If several wanted the same part, Mrs. Plotkin said, there would be try-outs. I crowded around the list with all the others. *Woodcutter*, it said; an *old woman; a rock; five soldiers; a bear; three daughters; seven dancing mice. . . .*

Beside each character it told what the requirements for the part would be. I searched the list for the three daughters:

Rosebud, Violet and Marigold: singing required.

My heart fell. I scanned the list again. I didn't want to be a bear or an old woman or one of the seven dancing mice. I didn't want to be part of the stage crew, either. I wanted to be Rosebud, Violet, or Marigold even more than I wanted Mrs. Plotkin's globe.

Tryouts were the following day, and I watched glumly as Elizabeth Price, Charlene Verona, and Pamela Jones walked off with the choice parts. I sat staring down at my knees.

"Alice," said Mrs. Plotkin, "I don't see your name here. What would you like to be?"

I knew I had to be something.

"A tree," I said.

While Pamela, Elizabeth, and Charlene were dancing around singing, I wanted to stand there with no expression whatsoever.

"A tree?" said Mrs. Plotkin, checking the list. "I don't see one listed, Alice. There's a bramble bush. How about that?"

I nodded.

Mrs. Plotkin studied me. "You're sure?"

"Yes," I said dryly. "All my life I've wanted to be a bush."

My one chance to be a star, and I couldn't take it because I couldn't sing. I thought about Momma and the way she used to sing songs from *Showboat*, the way Lester said. If she were alive, I'll bet she would have taught me. How could it be that things had suddenly started going all right in Mrs. Plotkin's room and now they were all falling apart again?

Wrapped in brown package paper, I stood miserably on stage while Pamela Jones, as Rosebud, waltzed back and forth in her long red dress, singing. When she wasn't on stage, she was off in the wings brushing her long blond hair, which had grown another inch since Halloween. I closed my eyes against my anger and disappointment.

There was one part in the play where Pamela and I were alone on the stage together. She was supposed to be lost in the woods and, in her fright, run directly into me. *The bramble bush, with branches thick,* said the playbook, *catches Rosebud and holds her fast.*

During the first rehearsal, I grabbed her sleeve. That was the rehearsal she stood right in front of me at the very end so no one could see my face. During the second rehearsal, I grabbed her shoulder. That was the rehearsal my wrapping paper ripped and she laughed. I was too angry to laugh, too angry to see the humor in anything. But the day of the pageant, in front of a hundred and sixty primary students, Pamela Jones stepped on my foot. Whether it was an accident or on purpose, I didn't know, but all the hatred I had felt toward her exploded at last. The bramble bush, with branches thick, grabbed her by the hair and yanked it hard.

Pamela shrieked, and suddenly, right there on stage, she yelled, "You did that on purpose, Alice McKinley!"

A gasp came from all the first-, second-, and third-graders there in the audience, followed by laughter. Pamela's face turned pink and so did mine, and suddenly she ran from the stage. I stood alone and embarrassed, listening to Pamela weeping off in the wings, and Mrs. Plotkin coaxing her to go back and finish the scene. I couldn't even walk in my brown paper wrapper so I couldn't go anywhere. Meanwhile the primary kids started talking and crawling all over each other, and the teachers were waving their arms, telling them to sit down.

After a lot more whispers from behind stage, Pamela Jones came back on, her face tear-streaked, and somehow we finished the play. But I knew that after all Mrs. Plotkin's work on the pageant, I had ruined it for her. The lump in my throat felt like a baseball.

I sat silently in the front seat of Mrs. Plotkin's car, trying to hold back the tears. The bell had rung, and everyone had left for Christmas vacation. We sat there so long I began to think my punishment was to spend the night in Mrs. Plotkin's car. But finally she said, "I don't think you feel very good about what happened, Alice."

I needed to talk, but only a little bit of the feelings came out—only a little of how awful, mean, and rotten Pamela was for trying to horn in on Mrs. Plotkin and me after school, only a part of how much I hated Pamela for getting to be Rosebud. The tears kept welling up and spilling over. On top of everything, I couldn't bear the thought that I had flubbed Mrs. Plotkin's play.

"It seems," Mrs. Plotkin said at last, "that you're angry at Pamela for wanting the very things that you want. It's not so horrible to want to be special, Alice."

I sat without moving.

She reached down and turned the key in the ignition, and the Chevy backed out of the space. "The thing is, no matter how many people are around, you are still very special." She smiled a little bit. "And whether you are a bush or a rosebud, Alice McKinley, doesn't make one bit of difference to me."

I swallowed. Maybe it didn't make any difference to her, but it did to me. There's a lot of difference between waltzing around the stage in a long red dress and standing up there in wrapping paper.

Mrs. Plotkin must have known where I lived, because the car took all the right turns. But when we reached my house, I didn't even try to open the car door. I just sat there gulping. Mrs. Plotkin turned off the motor.

"Sometimes," I said, "I worry . . . that I'm not growing up . . . at all." And as if that wasn't crazy enough, I added, "Sometimes I think I'm growing backward." Then the tears really poured.

It's strange, but all the while I was sitting there listening to myself cry, I was wondering what *I* would do if *I* were the teacher, what *I* would say to a bawling girl who thought she was growing backward.

What Mrs. Plotkin said was this: "We really don't have any choice, Alice. We grow up whether we're ready or not. It's just more difficult for some people than it is for others. I don't know about you, dear, but I just have a feeling that the new year is going to be better for you somehow. I really do."

I sniffled and gulped, and Mrs. Plotkin handed me a tissue. I wiped my nose without blowing. Lester says I sound like a truck when I blow, and I didn't want to make things worse than they were.

At last I got out of the car and went up the walk to the house. I opened the door without turning around and closed it without waving goodbye. Then, from behind the curtain, I watched Mrs. Plotkin drive off. I didn't feel good, but I didn't feel quite as bad as I did before. Mrs. Plotkin was giving me another chance, and no matter how many stupid things I'd done in her classroom, I knew she'd be glad to see me again after the first of the year.

11

Love

IT WAS a weird Christmas. Dad always feels low because he misses Momma, Lester was missing Marilyn; and I wasn't feeling very Christmasy myself. When Uncle Harold called from Tennessee to ask how we all were up here in "Silver Sprangs," Dad said, "Fine, just fine," and I thought how easy it was to fool yourself.

Mrs. Plotkin was right, and I knew it. I didn't like Pamela because she was trying to steal attention, the same attention I wanted for myself. It was the same with Charlene and Elizabeth Price. The harder they tried to be special to Miss Cole or Mr. Weber, the more I disliked them, because I was trying so hard myself. When I added up all the hateful things the girls had done or said to me, and then added up all the hateful looks I'd given them, I think we came out about even. Mrs. Plotkin saw right through me; she saw Alice McKinley at her worst, but she didn't stop liking me. Knowing that made the holidays bearable.

It was Janice Sherman at the Melody Inn who had helped me pick out a gift for Dad: a book about famous composers and the great loves of their lives. It wasn't till Dad opened it and said, "Hmmm!" that I got the terrible idea that maybe Janice Sherman was in love with my father and wanted to be *his* great love. Even worse, Loretta gave me a pair of jockey shorts to give to Lester. They had little snowmen all over them, and she said she got them in a package of three for her brother, and that I could have one for Lester. Then I began to worry that Loretta was getting ideas about him. I decided that if I ever came home and found that Dad had married the woman in sheet music and Lester was engaged to Loretta, I would hitchhike to Chicago and go live with my Aunt Sally.

I think we were all glad when the holidays were over and things sort of fell into place again. Most of the kids had forgotten the pageant and were friendly if I was. Pamela Jones still wasn't speaking, but I tried to take an interest in whatever Charlene and Elizabeth talked about at recess, and what they were talking about already was Valentine's Day.

Wasn't it sad, they said, that this year was probably the last time we'd ever make valentine boxes? When you get to junior high, they said, you don't get valentines anymore. I tried, but I couldn't feel the least bit sad about it. I remembered how back in Takoma Park one girl found a box of Whitman's chocolates stuffed in the slot of her valentine box, and while the rest of us took home a shoebox full of punch-out valentines from the dimestore, that girl was choosing between raspberry cremes and chocolate nougats from the chart on the lid of her Sampler.

It was February before I knew it. I couldn't think of a single idea for a card, so I asked Lester, and for once he was helpful. He said to cut out a bunch of white hearts from shirt cardboard, glue a stick of gum to each one, and write, "Valentine, I Chews You" in red pencil, so I did.

It was a dumb party. We had pink punch and little candies with things like "Hot Mama" and "Big Time" printed on them. We were allowed to give valentines to people in other classes, but I just slipped in Miss Cole's room long enough to put a valentine in her box, a white handkerchief from the Melody Inn with the notes to Schubert's Serenade printed in red. I gave the same thing to Mrs. Plotkin.

At three o'clock I picked up my decorated shoebox and went home, glad to have it over with. The hearts were falling off my box already because I'd just slopped them on and scribbled my name on the top.

Lester was reading on the couch.

"Hi," he said. "Nice party?"

"The pits," I told him, and went on up to my room.

I could tell there weren't a whole lot of valentines in my box, but at least it wasn't empty. I took off the lid and dumped them on my bed. There was the usual one from Mrs. Plotkin to all her students and some from kids I hardly knew. There wasn't any from Pamela Jones. But under all the others was one that just said

"Alice M." on the envelope and was decorated with little drawings of hearts and roses and airplanes with red stripes on their wings.

I opened the envelope. It was one of those misty-looking photographs of a man and woman walking through the woods holding hands and you can't see their faces. At the top, in curly letters, the words said, "A Special Feeling When I Think of You." I sat down on the bed.

There weren't any printed words on the inside of the card, but someone had taken a blue pen and written, "I like you a lot."

I dropped the card on the floor as though it were alive or something. When my heart stopped pounding, I gingerly picked it up by one corner and turned it over. There was no signature anywhere.

I looked at the envelope again. It had to be a boy who sent it. I didn't understand the airplanes; I figured he drew them because he wasn't so good at hearts and roses but wanted me to know there were some things he could draw. I looked at the card again, at the "special feeling when I think of you."

In spite of all the dumb things I'd done at Parkhaven Elementary, somebody still liked me, somebody besides Mrs. Plotkin.

It made going to school really creepy. I found myself looking at every boy in my class, wondering if he was the one. And then, because I was looking at him, he looked at me back, and by lunchtime half the boys in the room were shifting uncomfortably in their seats.

Every time I got up to sharpen a pencil or turn in a workbook, I'd take a long look at all the artwork above the blackboard to see if anyone had drawn airplanes. There were some pictures of boats and a racing car and a few Mack trucks, but no airplanes. When Mrs. Plotkin asked me to return the spelling papers, I checked to see which boy was using a pen with blue ink. Eight boys were using blue ink.

I began to carry a comb to school so I could untangle my hair at recess. I separated all my shirts with holes and buttons missing from the others and started wearing only the nicer ones to school. At recess I'd stand back by the fence and turn my face up to the sun the way I'd seen Miss Cole do and sort of let my hair tumble down my back, except that Dad keeps it cut short, so even when I tipped my head back all the way, my hair only reached my shoulder blades. Sometimes I'd stand at the fence the whole period, but no boys ever came over.

"Hey, McKinley, get out of the way!" somebody yelled during a soccer game, so I gave up posing by the fence and went back to talk to Charlene and Elizabeth.

Pamela Jones still wasn't speaking, however, and I decided I was going to have to make the first move. One Thursday, when I saw she wasn't going to stick around Mrs. Plotkin's room after school, I decided to leave with her and tried to start a conversation all the way to the corner.

"Did you do your book report yet?" I asked her.

Pamela just turned her head the other way.

"I'm reading *The Outsiders*," I told her. "It's a pretty good book."

Pamela kept walking.

We got to the corner and stood waiting for Patrick to give us the signal to cross.

"Pamela," I said, "are we going to go the rest of the year without speaking?"

Pamela just lifted her head a little higher and said, "Come on, Patrick, let us cross."

Patrick motioned us across the street, and I followed glumly along beside Pamela.

"Hey, Alice," Patrick said when I reached the other side.

I turned just in time to see a Milky Way fly through the air, and I caught it.

"You can have it," he said.

"Thanks," I told him, wondering. Maybe he was allergic to chocolate or something. I caught up with Pamela. "You want half?" I said. She looked down at it and didn't answer. I broke it in two and handed a piece to her. She started walking a little slower while she unwrapped it. A block later, she was listening to me. Two blocks later, we were talking. Three blocks later we were friends again, sort of.

The next day at school Miss Cole's class was decorating the hall for the sixth grade unit on communication. The class had done a mural that stretched all the way from the boys' rest room to the drinking fountain.

They had drawn all the ways that people communicate with each other. There were people talking on telephones and postmen delivering letters. There were pictures of trains carrying people to cities, airplanes carrying them coast to coast, and satellites in outer space. I bent over to get a drink of water, then suddenly straightened up. I looked at the airplanes again, and my heart thumped. They each had red stripes on the wings.

I stopped Charlene as she was going to class.

"Who drew the airplanes?" I asked her.

"Patrick," she said, and went on inside.

I knew that I could never cross his corner again without my hands starting to sweat. It was easier when I didn't know who had sent the valentine. Now that I did, what did I do next?

12

Eating Squid

ON THE WAY to school the next morning, Patrick threw another candy bar toward me, a Three Musketeers. This time I was so nervous I dropped it, and then I saw Patrick smiling and I smiled back; and after that, I guess, we were going together.

I really don't know what he saw in me. Patrick could have had almost anybody in sixth grade for a girlfriend, even gorgeous Elizabeth Price or Pamela Jones with her long blond hair. But then, how do you explain that Mrs. Plotkin is married and Miss Cole isn't? It doesn't make one bit of sense.

Patrick and I were about as different as two people could possibly be. *Nothing* embarrasses Patrick very much, and *everything* embarrasses me. Just being alive embarrasses me. After all the agony I went through over seeing Patrick in his underpants, I believe he never thought much more about it. It's strange now to think that he was one of the people I wanted to disappear or something because I'd seen him in his underpants, and what did he do? He wore them as part of his Superman costume at Halloween.

The day I dropped the Three Musketeers and we started going together, Patrick came over to my table at lunchtime and sat down beside me. While Elizabeth Price and Charlene and all the other kids stared, he just unwrapped his sandwich, asked me where I lived, and wanted to know if he could ride over sometime on his bike. Just like that.

"*Al*-ice, how's *Pa*-trick?" the girls would say every day.

"Fine," I'd answer, just like Patrick said it when they teased him about me. If you don't get all embarrassed and die over something, I discovered, teasing wears out after a while.

Sometimes, though, when Patrick sat on our porch railing, it was hard for me to think up things to talk about. Patrick *always* had something to talk about. Patrick had lived overseas. He'd lived in Germany and Spain and Japan, and every summer he flew out to Oregon by himself to spend vacation with his grandparents. The farthest I'd ever been was Tennessee. I'd never been on an airplane. I'd never even been on a train! Patrick could speak Spanish and count in Japanese. All I knew was pig-Latin. While he told me about eating squid in Hawaii, I told him about eating strained beets in Chicago. It was really pitiful.

One night at dinner, just after Dad had plunked a

pork chop on my plate, all I could think of was how Patrick's family ate squid.

"Why don't we ever have squid?" I grumbled, flopping my pork chop around on my plate like a dead chicken.

Dad paused between the stove and the table.

"Squid!" said Lester.

They both stared at me. I glared back.

"Why haven't I even been on a *train*?" I demanded.

Dad put down the frying pan. "Al, what the heck is eating you?"

I knew I wasn't making the least bit of sense. I swallowed. "Patrick's been everywhere," I mumbled.

"Who's Patrick?" asked Lester, still staring, and then his eyes lit up. "The new boyfriend, huh?"

I nodded. In order to have a new boyfriend you have to have had an old one; if Donald Sheavers counted as the old boyfriend, then I guess Patrick was number two.

"Well!" said Dad. "I see!"

"I've never *done* anything. I've never *gone* anywhere. I've never eaten squid, and I can't count in Japanese," I said in despair. "I am the most boring person in the whole world."

I mean, I really know how to ruin a mealtime. I felt guilty about it afterwards, too, and stayed in the kitchen to do the dishes. Then I went up to my room and pulled Saint Agnes out from under my mattress. It seemed perfectly dreadful that I should go around squalling about squid when little Saint Agnes had lost her head. I stuffed the card back under the mattress.

Pamela and I had been taking turns helping Mrs. Plotkin after school. Mrs. Plotkin said she really didn't need two girls helping out at once, so I came in Monday, Wednesday and Friday one week, and Tuesday and Thursday the next. Then one of the patrols resigned and Pamela was made a regular so she stopped helping out at all, and I had Mrs. Plotkin to myself again.

It's strange about Mrs. Plotkin, but she seemed to be changing. Sometimes, when I was cleaning the blackboard with my back to her, I realized that she had one of the most beautiful voices I'd ever heard. If you heard such a voice over the telephone, you would imagine a beautiful, slender woman in a long purple gown with orchids in her hair. Then I'd turn around and I'd see this large woman with the heavy legs . . . only somehow she looked prettier than she did that first day outside on the playground.

I wrote in my journal every day, just putting the words down as they came to me. Mrs. Plotkin said that all great writers wrote about subjects that really mattered to them, and that's why she wanted us to get used to writing about feelings, not just things. But one day something happened I would never put in my journal.

I was passing the school office during the lunch hour, and the secretary asked if I would take a note to Miss Cole. The garage had called, she said, and left an estimate for repairing Miss Cole's sports car. I knew that Mrs. Plotkin was on playground duty, so I figured the rest of the teachers were in the lounge.

I went down the hall and opened the door. Some of the teachers were eating lunch at the table. Miss Cole was taking her paper cup over to the trash.

"I wonder if I've got time to run to the bank," Mr. Weber was saying. "Who's on playground duty?"

In answer, Miss Cole turned toward him and let her shoulders droop, her arms dangle. She took a few steps forward, leaning heavily on one foot, then the other.

My hands felt chilly. I wished I hadn't seen that.

"Miss Cole," I said, "here's a note from the office."

She turned around. "Oh! I didn't see you, Alice. Thank you." She watched me leave.

I went quickly back out into the hall and closed the door behind me. I shut my eyes against what Miss Cole had done, but I couldn't get rid of the picture. I wanted to protect Mrs. Plotkin from it, however. I would never write it down in my journal.

At dinner that night there was squid. It was tough and yucky and I wondered why on earth Patrick would ever admit to eating anything so awful. Still, I knew I had to eat every bite.

But that wasn't all. When I had washed the last piece down, Dad said "I've got a little surprise for you, Al."

I didn't want any more surprises.

"How would you like to go to Chicago over spring vacation and visit your Aunt Sally?"

I didn't want to visit Aunt Sally. Chicago was not Hawaii or Spain or Japan. Before I could say no, however, Dad went on: "I've made a reservation for you on the Capitol Limited."

"The what?"

"It's a train, and you're going to have a roomette, your own little bedroom. It will be quite an experience! Aunt Sally will take you shopping for some new summer clothes, take you to the theater, to museums. . . ."

There was no way in the world I could say no. Three weeks later Dad drove me down to Union Station and saw me to the gate. He wanted to put me on the train himself and tell the conductor to look after me, but I wouldn't hear of it. Then *everybody* would know it was my first trip.

"You're going to have a great time, Al," he promised. "Something to talk about when you get back."

The crowd moved through the gate, and then I was walking along a silver and blue train, car after car after car, my suitcase banging against my leg.

13
Flushing on the Capitol Limited

I HAD HOPED I'd be assigned to the cheerful black porter who helped me on, but I got a grumpy-looking man instead with a face like mashed potatoes. For the first five minutes in my tiny roomette, I tried to find the toilet, but I certainly wasn't going to ask my porter. I found the closet and the cupboard and the ice water dispenser, but no toilet. Then I lifted the lid of the hassock and there it was, right in front of the window!

Everything is collapsible on a train—the bed, the sink, the chair. People are collapsible. On my way to the dining car, the train lurched and I fell right across the lap of a woman who was reading to her little boy.

"Get off!" the kid said, and pounded me on the ear.

At the table, while I was waiting for my cheeseburger, the train lurched again and the water in my glass spilled over onto the trousers of the businessman next to me who was enjoying his rock cornish hen with wild rice.

It took twice as long to get ready for bed as it did at

home because everything kept moving. The soap slid round on the edge of the sink, and everytime the train went around a bend, I'd go careening against the mirror. *Do not place valuables on sink*, said a little sign between the faucets, but I forgot and closed the sink up with the wash cloth still on it. When I opened it again, the cloth was gone, lying somewhere on the tracks between Pittsburgh and Canton, Ohio.

I had just used the toilet when the train stopped. There was another sign under the lid of the hassock: *Do not flush when train is in station*. I wondered what would happen if somebody flushed. I imagined people standing on the platform saying goodbye and suddenly a trap door opening under the train. Then I imagined the train going down the track at sixty miles an hour and everybody flushing. That didn't seem right either. I wondered when you could flush in an airplane. Maybe you had to wait till you were over the ocean or something.

While I was waiting for the train to start up again so I could flush, I studied the control panel just inside the door. I pushed a button, and a fan came on. I pushed another for the ceiling light. I kept going, right down the row, and then I realized I had called the porter.

I froze. Somewhere a light had lit or a buzzer had buzzed, and the man with the mashed-potato face would be on his way to number six. I pulled on my pajamas and curled up in the seat, with my arms over my head.

"Porter!" I heard the man call as he went up and down the aisle outside. "Porter!"

What would happen if I didn't answer? I wondered. Would they stop the train? Would they call the paramedics and blowtorch my door? But after a while he went away, the train started moving, I flushed, and I knew I was going to have to get the bed down by myself, because I couldn't possibly call the porter again.

There was a big handle on the wall over the seat so I turned it. The seat folded up and the wall started to come down on top of me. The bed was taking up the whole space! I would be crushed! *Silver Spring Girl Crushed by Bed on Capitol Limited*, the headlines would say.

When I was down on the floor, I realized that the bed had stopped falling and was resting on the hassock. I could just reach my hand up and open the door, crawl out inside the zippered curtain, climb up on top of the bed, and close the door again.

I settled down under the covers, my heart still pounding. It was dark now outside the window. I turned on my bed lamp and took my journal out of my suitcase. Mrs. Plotkin had asked us to keep it going during spring vacation, so I wrote about falling in that woman's lap back in the passenger car and how, if all the people who had ever seen me do something ridiculous were to die or disappear or something, hundreds would vanish off the face of the earth. Then I turned out the light and closed my eyes.

Suddenly I realized that the bed was rising. Just when I felt myself drifting off to sleep, my feet seemed to be higher than my head. The bed was closing! I was going to be buried alive! *Silver Spring Girl Suffocates on Capitol Limited!* I yanked my suitcase off the rack and put it on the bottom of the bed to hold it down. Then I had to go to the bathroom again. The 7-Up I'd drunk at supper was going through me like a rocket.

I put my suitcase on the rack, opened the door, stepped down behind the zippered curtain, lifted the bed till it hung suspended halfway up, and used the toilet. This time, when I lowered the bed, I saw a little sign on the wall that said, *Lock bed securely.* There was a latch on the wall and a latch on the bed. The latch clicked. The bed was secure. I finally went to sleep.

The next thing I knew, the conductor was calling, "*Chi*-cago! Chicago, Illinois!"

I couldn't believe it. I wasn't up! I wasn't dressed! I wasn't even awake!

Peeping out the window, I could see that we were entering a large city. I yanked down my suitcase and dressed on top the bed. I slid open the door, leaped down behind the curtain, pushed up the bed, and splashed water on my face. There was barely time to flush the toilet before the train stopped. Grabbing my toothbrush from the sink and my jacket from the closet. I crammed my pajamas into my suitcase and went out in the hall, dragging my suitcase after me.

I hadn't seen my aunt for six years, but I knew that the tall gray-haired woman in the red raincoat was Aunt Sally.

"They didn't wake me!" I explained, but she just swooped down with her long arms and hugged me to her, lifting my heels right up off the concrete.

"Alice McKinley, I can't *wait* to get you home and feed you!" she declared, and if I looked like the dog's breakfast, she didn't say so. She just picked up my suitcase with one hand and linked her other arm in mine and marched me right down the platform, through the Chicago terminal, and down the block toward a parking lot.

I liked Aunt Sally right away. She had that determined look in her eyes, like a woman in charge of her life; and at that point I wanted somebody to take charge of me. Maybe fate had sent me to Chicago; maybe now that boys were getting interested in me—Patrick, anyway—Aunt Sally was just what I needed. She was easy to talk to, and while she headed out to the suburbs, she told me about all the things we were going to do during my vacation.

"Your Uncle Milt is at work, but we'll have us a big dinner tonight," she was saying, "and of course Carol's coming by."

"Who's Carol?" The name seemed vaguely familiar.

Aunt Sally looked over at me. "Why, Alice, Carol's our daughter, your very own cousin. Don't you remember?"

"Oh, yeah. Right." I said, trying hard to think what she looked like.

"She married last year—husband's in the navy . . ."

Aunt Sally rattled on and on, and my eyes began to get heavy. I was about to fall asleep there on the front seat of her Pontiac when all of a sudden I straightened up and stared.

"Aunt Sally, you've got to stop!"

The brakes began to catch, and Aunt Sally swerved over toward the curb.

"What's the matter?"

I was looking at a church just beyond a Catholic school and playground. *Church of St. Agnes*, it said.

"I've just got to go in there," I told her, pointing.

The Pontiac stopped.

"Alice, have you turned Catholic?"

"No, but it's just something I have to do," I explained.

I could see that Aunt Sally didn't understand at all. "You're not dressed for church, Alice."

"*She* won't care," I insisted, knowing that a girl who had been put to death by the Romans could scarcely mind whether hundreds of years later another about-to-be-twelve girl had the proper clothes or not.

"You've nothing on your head!" Aunt Sally protested. She turned off the ignition and dug around in her purse until she found a plastic rain bonnet.

"Here," she said. "You've got to be decent."

I couldn't for the life of me understand how a plastic rain bonnet over uncombed hair was going to make me decent, but Aunt Sally meant business, so I put it on.

"I'll wait here," she said.

It was almost ten o'clock on a Saturday morning, and the church was empty. In the vestibule was a rack of free pamphlets about the Catholic Church, and one of them said, *Saint Agnes, Martyr*. I took it with me and walked slowly down the aisle toward the little statue off on one side.

There was no light in the church except what was coming through the stained glass windows and from the candles in front. But the statue of Saint Agnes looked just like the picture I had back home under my mattress.

I sat down on the pew next to the statue. Just like her picture, she was holding a lamb and a palm branch, and her bare feet pointed daintily out beneath her blue robes.

The pamphlet told how at the age of twelve, Agnes had consecrated herself to a heavenly husband. She had a lot of suitors who wanted to marry her, but she wouldn't give in, and so they accused her of being a Christian and she was sent to be judged. Still she wouldn't give in. "At last," the pamphlet said, "terrible fires were made, and iron hooks, racks and other instruments of torture displayed before her, with threats of immediate execution. The heroic child surveyed them undismayed, and made good cheer. . . ."

I swallowed and looked up at the statue again. Maybe *Agnes* had sent me here to Chicago, I was thinking. Maybe the girl with a dozen boyfriends, the girl who could laugh in the face of her persecutors, could be the model that Alice McKinley was looking for. Maybe, though I didn't see quite how, if I carried around her card when I got home, I wouldn't feel so awful when I did something stupid.

I stuffed the pamphlet in the pocket of my jacket and went back out. Aunt Sally started the car.

"Tonight," she said, not even looking at me, "I'm going to have Carol cut your hair."

14
Aunt Sally, Sir

EVERYTHING at Aunt Sally's is organized.

"A place for everything, and everything in its place," she said. She said it when she took me up to Carol's old room, and she said it when I came down to lunch, and she said it that evening to Uncle Milt when he left his umbrella on a chair instead of the stand.

Uncle Milt didn't seem to mind. "My Sally runs a tight ship," he said, when Aunt Sally was in the kitchen making supper. And when she called out to remind him to change the light bulb on the porch, he smiled, saluted, and said, "Yes, sir, Aunt Sally, sir."

Carol, their married daughter, came for dinner, and she looked exactly like Aunt Sally, only younger. She dressed in old sloppy clothes, but on Carol they looked great. Aunt Sally didn't seem to think so, but they did. Carol was tall and freckled the way I imagined my mother looked, and her eyes were always smiling even when her mouth wasn't.

"Wow," Carol said, when she walked in. "The last

time I saw you, Alice, you were five years old and blowing soap bubbles on our back porch."

"And not long before that. . . ." said Uncle Milt, smiling, "she was sitting at a high chair at this very table, and we were feeding her strained beets."

"And you were an absolute mess!" said Aunt Sally, but she was smiling too.

"She sneezed," said Carol, laughing. "Don't you remember? She had a mouthful of strained beets, and she sneezed."

"All over the table," said Aunt Sally. "The walls, the floor, the refrigerator. . . ." She was studying me again. "What can you do about her hair, Carol? Can't you cut it or something?"

I began to feel like an exhibit.

Carol looked at me. "You want me to give it a try? Taper the edges a little?"

"Sure," I said. "Why not?"

After dinner, while Aunt Sally did the dishes, I sat on the table while Carol cut my hair. Afterwards she showed me how to comb it back and fluff it up with the blow dryer.

"I've got next Tuesday off," she told me. "I'll show you around Chicago, all the places Mother's missed."

After Carol went home, I was feeling pretty tired and was glad when Uncle Milt suggested we all go to bed early. Aunt Sally followed me upstairs, though. She reached in the closet and pulled out a box.

"For you," she said. "For Easter. Your dad gave me your sizes."

"My gosh!" I said, pleased, but then I looked inside. There was a white dress, with white shoes and pantyhose. It was the kind of dress that southern girls wear for their coming-out parties, except that it only came down to my knees. There were ruffles on the shoulders and a flounce along the hem, and little white bows from the neck to the waist. I was speechless.

"Oh, try it on!" said Aunt Sally excitedly. "I just can't wait."

I tried not to look in the mirror when she slipped it over my head.

"For goodness sake, open your eyes!" Aunt Sally said. "Now if that isn't adorable!"

I did not look adorable. I looked like a vanilla cupcake with frosting running down over the sides. The only way I got to church on Easter Sunday was by reminding myself that I didn't know anyone and would never see any of them again.

We were all taking pictures of each other in the backyard later—Aunt Sally and me, Uncle Milt and me, me alone—when Carol came over.

"Oh, no!" she breathed, when Aunt Sally wasn't listening. "The Easter dress! I didn't know they made them like that anymore. Mother, poor dear, means well, Alice, she really does, but go upstairs and put on something comfortable."

It was strange being around Carol and Aunt Sally because they were so different. When Aunt Sally took me out for the day, she had a list all prepared of what we were going to do and see—where we were going to eat lunch, even. We started out at the aquarium. Then we did the Field Museum and the Planetarium and by the time we got back to the car I was positively crawling with weariness, while Aunt Sally hadn't even begun to get tired yet.

When Carol took me out on Tuesday, she didn't have anything planned. We just got on the el and rode and rode until we felt like getting off. We wandered around Buckingham Fountain and later went shopping at Marshall Fields. Carol bought me a pair of jeans that said *Hang Ten* on the bottoms, a striped shirt with slits at the sides, some rope sandals, an Indian print skirt, and my first bra. She even showed me how you bend over and sort of let yourself fall into it before you hook it in back. After that we ate stuffed grape leaves in a little Greek restaurant. Then we walked along Lake Michigan, swinging our packages, before we caught the el and came back home.

Aunt Sally believes that anything is possible. We were talking one morning about how it was being the only girl in a house with my dad and Lester, and Aunt Sally said that if girls have survived with only one lung or one leg, then I could survive with only one parent. All I had to do, she said, was figure out what I wanted most in the whole world and then make a plan for getting it. I told her what I wanted most in the whole world was a mother, so we were back to square one.

I liked Aunt Sally, though—*some* of the things about her, anyway. I liked the way she arranged her kitchen, with everything hanging on its own special hook on the pegboard. I liked the confident way she did things; but I liked Carol too—her easy-going manner, so different from her mother's. Aunt Sally would never wear anything that said *Hang Ten*. She would never wear any clothes with words on them, she told me, because she was a woman, not a billboard. It was possible, I discovered, to like two people who were entirely different.

Nice as they were, though, sometimes at night I felt a little homesick. Once Aunt Sally must have noticed because she asked if I wanted to call home. But I really didn't feel I needed to talk to my father. I certainly didn't need to talk to Lester. I just didn't know what it was.

On Thursday night I awoke about midnight, my abdomen aching. I turned over and felt something sticky between my legs. Turning on the bed lamp, I peeped inside my pajamas. I let the elastic snap and lay back down, staring wide-eyed at the ceiling. Then I sat up and peeked again. I was menstruating.

I put on my robe and looked for some Kotex in the bathroom. Then I tried the hall closet.

Aunt Sally's door opened and she came out.

"Alice?" she said, shielding her eyes from the light. "What's wrong?"

"Nothing," I said. "I guess I need some Kotex."

Aunt Sally dropped her hand and stared at me. "Really? Is this your first time?"

"Yep," I said.

"Oh, Alice!" Aunt Sally knelt right down on the floor and put her arms around me. "Your very first time! My, such an occasion—the beginning of all the privileges and responsibilities of womanhood!"

That was really weird, and I didn't know what to say. I didn't want any privileges of womanhood. I just wanted some sanitary napkins.

Aunt Sally found them for me.

"Oh, I'm so *happy* you were here when it happened!" she went on. "Are you having cramps? Is there anything more I can do?"

I wanted to tell Aunt Sally to just go back to bed, please, but I thanked her and said I could manage, and finally she left me alone. Maybe that was the way mothers always acted, I thought. I just didn't know.

The next morning at breakfast there were flowers on the table. Store-bought flowers. Somebody had gone out and bought them.

"For you," said Aunt Sally proudly. "A special bouquet for our little moth who has become a butterfly."

I stared. Uncle Milt was beaming shyly, his eyes on his plate. Then he looked at Aunt Sally, and they beamed at each other.

She'd told him. I never felt so ridiculous in all my life.

15

Something for the Orphans

THE LAST DAY before I left Chicago, Aunt Sally and Uncle Milt showed me everything I hadn't seen before. We made it through the Museum of Science and Industry and the Art Institute before Uncle Milt said, "Good grief, Aunt Sally, sir, give the girl a rest."

We ate at a restaurant on the near-north side while Aunt Sally made a list of all the things we'd save for the next time I came to visit.

On Saturday, Carol drove me to the station, and I told her all about sleeping in a roomette and how you're not supposed to flush in the station and she laughed. She laughs a lot. I didn't even know I was funny till I met my cousin Carol. When we got to the gate, I hugged her hard, even harder than I'd hugged Aunt Sally, and that surprised me. I mean, when I started out for Chicago, I didn't even know I *had* a cousin named Carol.

This time, when I got on the train, I was an old pro. I knew exactly where the toilet was and how to latch the bed. The nice surprise was that Eddie, the cheerful porter, was on the train again, and this time I was assigned to him. He was in a joking mood:

"Well, look who we got with us again!" he said, hoisting my bag up on the rack above the mirror. "Another little gal for the orphanage."

"What?" I said.

"You didn't know this was a special train, dumps all little gals through a chute in Ohio? Great big old orphanage right there by the track, and we just send 'em down the chute one at a time, train hardly even has to stop." He winked at me and started to leave, then stuck his head back in: "I saw what happened to you in Chicago; they never even woke you up. You just tell me what time you want to get up for Washington, and I'll make sure you're ready."

This time I made it to the dining car without hardly wobbling. I still had ten dollars left for food, so I ordered the rock cornish hen, and sat in the club car afterwards with a very small 7-Up.

Eddie sat down with me for a few minutes and talked about his family, his four children, the oldest just about as old as me. And somehow I began to feel that strange kind of homesickness again. It wasn't quite so bad this time, because I was on my way home, so I tried to get in touch with my feelings, the way Mrs. Plotkin tells us to do in our journals. And suddenly I knew what the trouble was: I was homesick for Mrs. P.

Back in my roomette, I leaned against the window

and watched the lights speed by outside. I liked Aunt Sally, and I wanted to be confident of myself the way she was. I liked Carol too, and I wanted to be easy-going like her. I liked Lester's old girlfriend Marilyn, and I wanted to look and dress like Miss Cole when I got older. But while I wanted to look and laugh and dress like lots of different people, I wanted to *be* like Mrs. Plotkin. I wrote in my journal for a long time, even though the train made my handwriting wobbly.

The next morning, I knew I wasn't going to put on that white dress for anything in the world, even though Aunt Sally had said she wanted me to be wearing it to show Dad what a lovely young lady I had become. I knew, in fact, that I would never wear that dress again, and it would just turn yellow in my closet.

"You still here?" Eddie asked when he brought me some hot chocolate. "I thought sure you was one of those little gals we sent off down the chute last night in Ohio. Orphanage going to be mighty mad."

I put on my jeans that said "Hang Ten" and my striped shirt with the slits on the sides and my rope sandals. Then I left my white shoes and pantyhose in the closet under the dress and stuck a note to Eddie over the dress hanger:

Dear Eddie: Please give these clothes to one of the girls in the orphanage. Alice M. I knew that if there was any kind of orphanage at all, Eddie would take that dress to them, and if there wasn't, he'd find someone who wanted to look like a cupcake.

It was Lester, not Dad, who was waiting for me in Washington. He took my suitcase and gave me a hug. "Have a good time?"

"It was different," I told him.

"You get to see Carol? She still a good-looker?"

"I didn't even remember her," I told Lester. "But she's nice. I liked them all, but in different ways."

Lester talked to me like a human being on the way home. He told me that he was dating a new girl named Crystal Harkins, and that she was a real dish. I was glad to hear he hadn't taken up with Loretta.

I was beginning to feel good about being home again. I had a new haircut and some new clothes, and *Lester* even told me I looked smashing.

Dad hadn't come home from work yet, and the first thing I did when I got inside was call Mrs. Plotkin. I didn't even know what I was going to say. I just knew I had to call her, so I dialed before I could think too hard about it.

"Mrs. Plotkin," I said eagerly, "I'm home." And then I realized she hadn't even known I'd been away.

But somehow she recognized my voice. "Alice," she said, "wherever you've been, I'm really glad that you're back."

And then, as we were making dinner, the phone rang. Dad lifted the receiver off the wall with one hand and continued to jab at the meatballs with the other.

"Sally!" he said. "Well, what a surprise!"

I looked up.

"She says she had a *fine* time!" Dad went on. There was a pause, and I saw Dad frown just a little. "Did I like what she was wearing?"

My heart sank, and Dad and I stared at each other. Then I nodded my head violently, begging Dad with my eyes.

"Why, yes, Sal, she looked absolutely beautiful!" Dad said, taking his cue, and I sank down on a kitchen chair, one hand on my chest.

"Just beautiful," he said again. "I'm sure she's going to wear those clothes for a long time."

I fanned myself with a napkin.

"Okay," Dad said, when he hung up. "What'd you do with the white ruffled dress and the white shoes and pantyhose?" His voice was gruff, but he was smiling.

"Gave them to an orphanage," I said, "and some little gal is going to be mighty glad to get them."

When we sat down to dinner, Dad and Lester seemed quieter than usual. Quiet and polite. Lester even said "thank you" when I passed the rice. I knew then that Aunt Sally must have called home during the week and told them something else.

"Well, Al, I understand that this was quite a growing-up experience for you," Dad said at last.

"Yeah," I said. "I started my periods. So what else is new?"

16
Who Got the Globe

PATRICK didn't go anywhere over spring vacation. I thought he would have gone to India or something, but all he did was clean out their garage. He came over after supper the night I got back and sat on the porch railing while I told him about sleeping on the Capitol Limited. Would you believe that Patrick had never slept on a train? He'd never heard of cornish hen, either, and wanted to know if it was anything like squid.

"Better," I told him.

By the first of May, everyone started talking about how there were only a few more weeks left of school. I was pretty sure what Pamela Jones was thinking; she had her mind set on Mrs. Plotkin's globe, because she started making all A's on her geography tests, one right after another. She even knew the capitol of Nigeria. When we had to write essays for English, I wrote about sleeping in a roomette on the train and got an A. Pamela wrote about the Amazon River and got an A+.

I don't know if I wanted Mrs. Plotkin's globe because it was probably the nicest thing she was likely to give away or whether I just didn't want Pamela to have it. I think mostly it was that I wanted Mrs. Plotkin to show me that I was special. Something more than writing notes in the margins of my journal. More than the talks we had after school.

"You know, Al," Dad said to me one evening when we were making tacos. "You seem more mellow these days. You actually appear to be going off each morning to school, not to war." He smiled at me. "What did it? That visit with Aunt Sally?"

I shrugged. "I just get along better at Parkhaven, I guess."

"Good." He opened a can of refried beans and dumped them in on top of the ground beef, and then I added the green chili peppers. "I guess I've worried some about what growing up without a mother might do to you," he added.

I could tell he wasn't quite through worrying yet. Even fathers have to be reassured now and then.

"I'm not planning to run off with some guy on a motorcycle or anything," I told him. Then I couldn't help but add, "As long as you don't run off with Janice Sherman."

The spoon in Dad's hand paused in midair. "Whatever gave you that idea?"

"The way she looked at you at Thanksgiving."

He laughed. "Well, I'm certainly in the market for a wife, but you can bet it won't be her."

"There aren't any perfect women, though, Dad," I said, and then I couldn't believe I'd said it. *Alice the Wise.*

"Well, I'm not perfect either, so I don't worry much about that," he told me.

On the fourteenth of May, my birthday, something happened that if I had known back in September would happen, I would have looked forward to it all year. It was Miss Cole's birthday, too. The safety patrol decided to give her a surprise party after school, after all the patrols were off duty, and I waited in Mrs. Plotkin's room until I heard the regulars coming back. Then I slipped down the hall just in time to burst in with the others, all yelling, "Happy birthday!"

But there, on the big store-bought cake with yellow roses, it said in frosting, *Happy Birthday Miss Cole and Alice.*

"I remembered," Charlene said, smiling at me across the cake. I never thought she would do anything so nice.

"Why, Alice, is this your birthday, too?" Miss Cole said, and she came around the cake and hugged me close to her apricot-colored blouse. I could smell the perfume on her skin.

It's funny that sometimes what you think you want more than anything in the world is okay when it happens, but not all that great. I could feel myself blush. I loved having Miss Cole's arm around my shoulder, but I didn't cry with joy or anything. We sat on top of the desks eating the chocolate cake and laughing, and Patrick took the two yellow roses off his piece and let me have them.

All the while we were eating, though, I was thinking about Mrs. Plotkin back in her room, making up tomorrow's lessons, and wondered if anybody had ever given her a birthday cake with yellow roses.

Miss Cole didn't seem in any hurry at all to send us home. She told us about the best birthday she'd ever had —when she was twenty-one and her father gave her a car—and the worst birthday—when she was seven and had chickenpox. Everyone was laughing and telling his own tales of best and worst birthdays, and finally I got down off the desk and said I had some work to do.

"Then take a big piece of that cake with you, Alice." Miss Cole smiled, and she even cut it for me and wrapped it in a napkin.

I went down the hall to Mrs. Plotkin's room. She was standing at the blackboard in her green dress writing tomorrow's assignments. She moved slowly as she stepped back and forth, her hand pausing every now and then while she thought what to write next.

I set the cake on her desk.

"I guess it's my birthday," I said at last, which sounded so dumb you wouldn't believe. She turned around and looked at me.

"Well, for goodness sake, Alice, is that what all that singing was about?"

"Only half of it," I said. "It's Miss Cole's birthday, too. But I wanted you to have some of the cake."

"It looks simply delicious. I'd like to take it home and share it with Ned," she said.

My first thought was that Ned was a dog, and then I remembered she had a husband. Ned. Ned Plotkin. I tried to imagine a man named Ned Plotkin falling in love with this large woman standing between the desk and the blackboard. I found I could imagine it very well.

THE DAY BEFORE Mr. Weber's class left on the overnight, Elizabeth Price got a fever of a hundred and three and couldn't go. Life is really strange sometimes. You never know what's around the corner.

Mrs. Price was out sweeping the walk the next morning when I went to school.

"Is Elizabeth any better?" I asked.

"No," her mother told me. "The doctor says it's only the flu, but I've never seen her so disappointed."

I knew about disappointment, all right. When I got to Parkhaven, the bus was loading up with Mr. Weber's students, all carrying sleeping bags and lunches and shouting to each other and saving seats. I thought about Elizabeth all day, and when I got home, I pulled the Saint Agnes card out from under my mattress.

It wasn't that I felt I didn't need Saint Agnes anymore. I needed all the help I could get. It was just that Saint Agnes meant something special to Elizabeth, the way Mrs. Plotkin was special to me, and I knew it was wrong for me to keep the card, especially since it was probably Elizabeth's in the first place.

I walked across the street.

"Do you think I could see Elizabeth for a minute?" I asked. "I just want to say hello."

"Of course, but don't get too close in case it's catching," her mother said, and I went on upstairs.

Elizabeth's room smelled of orange juice and throwup. Elizabeth was lying on her pillow with her hair all stringy, and she didn't look much like the photograph on her living room wall.

"Hi," I said.

She turned her head. "Hi," she said weakly.

"I just came over to see how you were feeling."

"Yukky," Elizabeth said in answer.

I handed her the card. "I found this . . ." I began. "I thought maybe you'd lost it or something."

Elizabeth stared at the card, then took it.

"I lost this months ago!" she said.

"Well, I've had it for months," I apologized. I couldn't think of any other way to explain it, and Elizabeth was too weak to ask.

"Thanks," she said, and put it under her pillow.

I tried to think of something comforting to say. All I could think of was, *Cheer up. Saint Agnes didn't get to go on an overnight, either*, but that didn't sound right, so I just kept quiet.

"Did you see the bus leave?" Elizabeth asked.

I nodded.

"Just my luck," she said.

"Oh, sometimes things aren't as wonderful as you think they're going to be," I told her. "They'll probably all come back with chiggers and poison ivy."

She smiled a little. "Thanks for coming, Alice," she said.

WE ALL turned in our journals on June 1. Mrs. Plotkin said she'd give them back later, because she hoped we would want to go on writing in them for a long time. *It gets you over the rough places*, she said once.

I thought about that as I walked to school. I knew that a lot of what I'd written were things I would have told Momma if she were alive. I wouldn't have thought that just writing feelings down on paper could help much, but it did.

What I really wanted to do was write something to Mrs. Plotkin on the last page. I'd even thought about writing a poem, but then I remembered the verse I wrote the milkman, and knew that next year I'd probably look back on this one as just another agony. Everything I thought of to say sounded ridiculous, like the greeting cards that begin:

Although your leaving makes me sad,
Although our paths will part. . . .

and you already know that when you get to the fourth line, it's going to end with "heart."

When I got to class, I saw that some of the girls had written poems, though, and one had even drawn blue roses around the border.

I sat clutching my journal while Mrs. Plotkin checked attendance. What could I possibly write that would show how I felt about her now? Coming back from Chicago, I had written about feeling homesick, but it didn't seem enough. It didn't really show her how much I had changed.

Then suddenly I knew what to do. I could hear all the notebooks slapping together as they were passed forward up the rows. When they got to my desk, there was a five-second wait while I removed all the paperclips from my pages. I wanted Mrs. Plotkin to know that there wasn't anything I couldn't share with her now, the angry feelings as well as the good ones. When I finally put my journal on top of the others and passed them on, I saw Mrs. Plotkin smiling at me, the kind of smile you could take home and keep all year. I smiled back.

I never knew if she read those early pages or not. *It's all right to have secrets,* she'd told us once, *as long as you don't have any secrets from yourself.* When I got my journal back a few days later, she hadn't written anything about the first pages. She just wrote something at the end about how glad she was to have me in her classroom and how the 'agonies' I wrote about were things that happened to us all.

I wondered if that was true, if people went on doing stupid things even after they reached twenty. Yep, I decided. They just didn't worry about them so much, that's all.

On the last day of school, I waited until most of the others had left, laughing and yelling, the way they always do. Pamela Jones was there by the globe, turning it around and around on its squeaky pedestal.

"Anybody interested in a half jar of paste?" Mrs. Plotkin said. "It will only dry up over the summer." One of the boys took the paste and went off smiling.

A pair of scissors went next, with one point missing, and in a few minutes, Pamela and I were the only two left in the room with Mrs. Plotkin.

"Well, my special helpers!" Mrs. Plotkin said. She looked first at me and smiled, and then at Pamela. My heart began to thump.

"You know, Pamela, that globe is simply not going to last another year, I'm sure; and if you like, you can have it," Mrs. Plotkin said. Pamela's face lit up like a neon sign while my stomach did a dive.

"Really? Oh, Mrs. Plotkin, I've *always* wanted a globe! It's just the most wonderful thing . . !" She went on and on, and Mrs. Plotkin smiled at her as though I wasn't even there.

Part of me wanted to leave. Part of me wanted to clobber Pamela. But another part of me told me I loved Mrs. Plotkin for more than her globe. I stayed.

I filled the bucket with water for the blackboard and

began to scrub. Pamela chattered on about where she was going to put the globe, and Mrs. Plotkin sat at her desk cleaning out drawers. Finally, however, there was quiet in the room. Pamela had gone. I went on with the scrubbing, knowing it was the very last time I would clean Mrs. Plotkin's blackboard. I promised myself I wouldn't cry.

"Alice," Mrs. Plotkin was saying, "I don't have any children of my own, you know. . . ." I turned.

"I don't even have any nieces, just nephews," she said. She was smiling. Then she reached for her purse and opened it. "I don't know if you want this or not, but . . . you see, my great-grandmother passed it down to her daughter, who passed it down to my mother, and I was supposed to give it to *my* daughter, which I never had. . . ."

She took out a tiny box of gray velvet and opened it. There was a ring—a very old ring—with a large green stone in it about the color of Mrs. Plotkin's dress. The silver was very worn, and the green stone had a tiny chip on one side, but the next thing I knew Mrs. Plotkin was slipping it on one of my fingers—the finger with the cut on the knuckle and the dirt under the nail. Mrs. Plotkin didn't seem to notice, though. She held out my hand and looked at the big ring wobbling around on my finger.

"Well, now"—Mrs. Plotkin smiled—"I think my great-grandmother—she would have been your great-*great*-grandmother—would have been pleased to see who got this ring, Alice. I really do."

I couldn't even talk. I just threw my arms around Mrs. Plotkin's neck, and she hugged me back. I swallowed and swallowed, but I didn't cry.

Then we talked about what we were going to do over the summer, and Mrs. Plotkin told me how she was going to spend July in Vermont with Ned, and all the while I went on cleaning the blackboard, my eyes on the big green ring there on my finger. It was the most beautiful thing I had ever owned in my life.

Patrick came over that evening and brought me a miniature pack of Whitman's chocolate-covered cherries, but he'd left them in the sun all afternoon and we had to eat them with spoons. We sat side by side on the glider, our spoons poised over the melted chocolates. I'd scoop up one, then he'd take one, and when we were through eating, I knew he was going to kiss me.

There are some things you just sort of know. It got real quiet on the porch for one thing, and I realized that I was the only one pushing the glider. Out of the corner of my eye I could see him looking at me, and I knew that any minute he was going to lean over.

The old Donald Sheavers panic rose up in my chest, and my palms started to tingle. I was trapped. There wasn't even a sheet of cardboard to roll off of.

Alice McKinley, I told myself, *you can giggle and squirm and fall off the swing, or you can just get it over with.*

Patrick leaned a little further until I could smell the chocolate on his lips. The next thing I knew the glider was moving again, and Patrick was looking straight ahead. The boy who had lived in Spain and eaten squid had lost his nerve.

I wanted him to know that it was all right, so I started talking about everything I could think of—how Dad was going to rent a cottage at Bethany Beach over the summer, and how Lester's new girlfriend, Crystal Harkins, played the clarinet. But when I ran out of things to say, I knew that Patrick would try again. He fidgeted until he had one arm on the back of the glider just behind me, and the next time he leaned forward, he had his eyes closed, so I closed mine, and our lips collided. It was probably the shortest kiss in recorded history, but I knew that later that evening I would go upstairs, take out the poster, and write, "Kissed Patrick," in the *Forward* column. And Patrick seemed so relieved that I wondered if somewhere he wasn't keeping a list of accomplishments too, and that underneath "Count in Japanese," he would add, "Kissed Alice."

I guess he'd been so nervous about the chocolates and the kissing that he hadn't noticed the ring before, but suddenly his eye caught sight of it there on my finger, with adhesive tape wrapped around it on the palm side to keep it from falling off.

"Where'd you get the ring?" he asked, and for a moment I thought maybe he was jealous, that maybe he thought I had another boyfriend. I tried to imagine what it would be like to have two boys crazy over me at the same time. Three, even. Three boys all pining for me on the porch, and Lester having to run them off with the garden hose.

"It was passed down from a great-great-grand-mother," I told him.

"Looks good on you," Patrick said, "but it's sort of big, isn't it?"

I held my hand out in front of me, remembering the way Mrs. Plotkin had held it as she admired the ring. I smiled.

"I'll grow into it," I told him.